KNOX

complete series

CASSIA LEO

KNOX: COMPLETE SERIES
by Cassia Leo

First Edition

Copyright © 2014 by Cassia Leo

All rights reserved.

Cover art by Cassia Leo

Interior design by Angela McLaurin, Fictional Formats

ISBN-13: 978-1500299293
ISBN-10: 1500299294

KNOX

volume 1

CASSIA LEO

1

"OH, MARCO, DON'T stop."

His blue eyes are fixed on mine as he grinds into me, penetrating me deeper with each thrust. He's smiling at me. Oh, how I love that smile. I close my eyes and imagine the first time I saw that smile. Sitting in a booth in the corner of the shop. My father's arm around his shoulders, congratulating him.

"I've missed you, Marco."

I slide my hand behind his neck and pull his mouth against mine. It feels just like our first kiss, only better. We're older now. Wiser. I work for the department and Marco, he....

What does Marco do for a living?

"I love you, Marco. Tell me you love me."

He smiles as he kisses the corner of my mouth, but he doesn't say anything. I rake my fingers over his back and he doesn't make a sound. Not a hiss of air through his teeth or a soft moan. Nothing.

"Marco, please."

His cock is so thick, stretching me as he lifts my leg and pierces me slowly. I wrap my other leg around his hip, beckoning him further inside. Gasping, I throw my head back and he kisses the hollow of my throat. Ecstasy. This is pure, ethereal ecstasy. Dream-like. He slides his hand between us to caress my clit and my body quakes beneath him.

"I'm going to come, Marco. I'm coming! I'm coming!"

A soft chuckle wakes me and I find August next to me. The room is dark and I'm holding his hand prisoner between my thighs. A searing heat creeps up my cheeks as I realize I was dreaming about Marco again.

"Did you come?" August says, and I can hear the smug grin in his voice.

I push his hand back then turn around to face away from him. "Sorry."

He slides his arm around my waist and presses his chest against my back. "Goodnight, Becky."

2

"When was the last time you two went on a date?" Lita asks as we cross Vanderbilt.

A jerk in a silver hatchback blares his horn at us. Aren't hatchback drivers supposed to be stereotypically nice?

Lita and I pause on the corner of 42nd and Vanderbilt, Grand Central Terminal. I make a move to hug her goodbye and she laughs.

"Nuh-uh. Answer my question, Becky. When was the last time you and August went on a date?"

Her light-brown hair is a bit frizzy and her top lip is sweating from the sticky night air. She still manages to look gorgeous, like she just stepped off a photo shoot at an exotic location. Like she's been spritzed and primped to look exactly this way. Lita hates when people tell her she looks like a model. She actually thinks it's an insult. She desperately wants to be taken seriously. She gets this from working on Wall Street where her model stature and smooth voice must command notice.

"We're not dating. We're in a relationship. Date nights are for married couples trying to revive their relationship. There's nothing wrong with August and me. We're solid."

"Solid as the wall between you. When was the last time you went to his apartment?"

I want to launch into my usual spiel, but I'm actually afraid of how many times I've said the words aloud.

August and I have a comfortable relationship. We don't need to cling to each other every second of every day to feel secure. August loves me. I know that because he remembers my birthday and my favorite ice cream flavor. He knows how many kids I want (two, he wants four). And the biggest plus of all: he's not afraid to talk about marriage. He loves that I want a big wedding. And as soon as his blog is established enough that he can take more time off, we're getting married.

This is the part where you begin wondering if I'm actually this naïve. I'm not. I'm far from naïve. I may be a midtown girl now, but I was born and raised in Bensonhurst.

Born and raised in Bensonhurst. Whenever someone hears this phrase, they automatically assume I must be related to a crime family. Some people are brazen enough to come right out and ask me—in a joking manner, as if that makes the question less inappropriate. I just chuckle and say something like, "Wouldn't that be cool if I was?" That's what people want to hear.

People don't want to know the truth. They don't want to know that I left my entire family behind at the age of eighteen, except for the occasional phone call to my mother. They don't want to know that I chose a job in law enforcement with the hopes of sending my family a message. That message: I want nothing more to do with them. They especially don't want to know the things I've seen. Because people who idolize the mafia actually think that being the daughter of a crime boss is glamorous.

They imagine me in my fur coat, diamond encrusted fingernails. Maybe I'm dangling a designer handbag from my arm, stuffed with an adorable teacup Chihuahua. They imagine men who aren't afraid to get their hands bloody, coming home and using those same hands to rip off my lacy panties and claim me. They imagine a sexy, sinful cocktail of glamor spiked with a large dose of unyielding power.

For the most part, they're right. But they still haven't seen what I've seen. And what I saw in my living room, at the tender age of thirteen, was my father strangling a man I had come to know as Uncle Frank. A crime for which he was never punished, despite the many times my father has been in and out of jail for pettier crimes. The truth is that I barely know my father. I hope that never changes.

I look into Lita's wide gray eyes and I lie. "I was at August's apartment last week." I clap her arm awkwardly. She shakes her head so I lean in to hug her goodbye. "Enjoy your trip to Poughkeepsie. I'm sure your mom will have plenty of potato salad and honey-glazed ham to fatten you up."

"Don't rub it in."

She releases me and her fingers glance over my forearm as she walks away. As I watch her set off toward Grand Central Terminal, all I can think is that I *am* naïve. I am *so* naïve. I haven't been to August's apartment in four months.

I spin around to face the street and flag down the first cab. I'm going to August's apartment. I'm going to demand to know what is wrong with us. I'm twenty-three years old with a gorgeous twenty-five-year-old boyfriend who never takes me to his apartment. I know what he's going to say. He's going to say it's because I prefer midtown to the lower east side. Avoiding his apartment is just his way of trying to be agreeable. I'm not falling for that.

I throw my arm out angrily, determined to hail a cab and fly to August's apartment on a wind of fury. But the first car that stops for me is not a taxi. It's a shiny black SUV. And before I can step aside to try to hail a real cab, a man appears at my side, his fingers discreetly curling around my wrist.

"Your car is here." His dark eyes are locked on mine, never blinking, not even as the SUV door is flung open. "Your father needs to speak to you."

That's all he has to say.

3

I CLIMB INTO the SUV and I'm not surprised to find that there's another man in there waiting to receive me. Both he and the guy who met me on the curb are wearing dark suits and sunglasses. I'm sure if I could see anything inside this dark SUV, I'd find earpieces shining inside their ears.

When all three of us are settled into the backseat, the SUV pulls away from Grand Central Terminal and sets off down 42nd. The bigger guy on my left reaches behind his back and my heart stops. They wouldn't kill me just like that, would they? I brace myself for whatever he's about to retrieve from behind his back, my body tensed and ready to flail about. But when he pulls his hand out, he's holding a large piece of black cloth. Upon further inspection, I notice it's a black hood.

I can't see his eyes through the sunglasses, but the fact that he's offering it to me instead of putting it on me himself seems to be some show of respect. They're not going to kill me. They don't even want to hurt me. They're too afraid of my father. Which means that my father is not as angry with me for abandoning the family as I had imagined. Or... he wants something.

I huff as I snatch the black silk hood out of his hand. I quickly note my surroundings before I pull it over my head. We're just approaching Fifth Avenue. Everything goes black and I try to keep track of the many turns the vehicle makes. But it doesn't take long for me to realize that they're probably taking me on a winding route just to confuse me.

When the car finally stops and the engine dies, my stomach vaults. I haven't seen my father in four years since the last time I visited Mom at home and he was actually home—a rare occasion. I was nineteen and terribly homesick during Spring Break at Hunter College where I was studying, of all things, creative writing. My visit home was supposed to be soothing and relaxing and familiar. Instead, my father decided to get out of jail three weeks early and I left the house without him uttering a word to me; his eyes watching me as I walked out the door, his lips unable to break a smile or silence for his only child.

The worst part about leaving home is the conversations with my mother. She's had to endure my father's grief over the fact that she never gave him more than one child. She's never admitted it, but I can imagine him calling her useless. My mother is far from useless. Without my mother, I'd probably be traipsing around town with diamond-encrusted fingernails and a designer dog. My mother taught me to want more.

But I must admit that, as they help me out of the SUV and my heart pounds so hard I can barely breathe, it's not just fear of my father that has me this stressed. I'm also intrigued. For my father to have me essentially kidnapped and forced to meet with him, he must be desperate.

My summer sandals crunch on the gravelly pavement as someone grips my forearm and guides me forward. A door creaks open and I'm blasted with a cool gust of air-conditioned air. The smell of rubber and grease stings the inside of my nostrils as I'm pulled farther inside this new environment.

The whoosh of another door opening.

More walking.

Stop.

Is he here?

Silence.

"Brace yourself, kid." This warning issued by the guy on my right feels more ominous than it should. It's just my father in there, isn't it?

The silk hood is slipped off my head and we're standing in the middle of a wide garage with hydraulic lifts and tires and an assortment of equipment for repairing cars. But there are no cars in this garage. One person stands about ten feet away from me, facing me.

And it's not my father.

4

HIS DARK SUIT is perfectly tailored to his athletic body. He stands straight, with his arms clasped behind his back. His smooth skin and the shadow of hair along his jawline scream perfectionist. But the gleam in his blue eyes is deadly. It's a look that could make me divulge my darkest secrets. Like what I saw in my living room ten years ago.

His gaze slides from my face, downward, examining every inch of my body. None of his buffoons searched me for weapons, but they don't need to. And he knows that. His eyes settle on mine again and I see a hint of a smile curling his lips. And, what gorgeous lips they are. The perfect peaks and fullness with just a hint of natural sheen.

What is wrong with me?

This guy practically kidnaps me and I'm fantasizing

about his perfect skin and his lips. I'm clearly in shock or something. Especially when his lips have got *nothing* on his electric blue eyes.

"Do you know who I am?"

His voice is limber and gruff all at once; a low growl wrapped in silk. I open my mouth to speak and find that I'm not breathing. I draw in a deep breath then clear my throat. He looks impatient with me already.

"No."

I don't offer anything else. No desperate pleas for my release or indignant demands to know what is going on. Something tells me this guy has seen both of those reactions a thousand times. And he's not easily swayed.

His perfect dark hair flutters a bit under the air conditioning as he slowly walks toward me. I glance behind me; a nervous reaction. That's when I realize we are all alone. The two guys in the car have left the garage.

"Do you know why you're here?"

I want to say, *"Because you're an asshole,"* but that would be far too self-indulgent.

"No."

He raises an eyebrow and that tiny hint of a smile widens just a bit. "One-word answers. Your father taught you well."

Suddenly, my blood is boiling. My father didn't teach me squat. And I want to remind this guy of that. Until I remember that my father *did* teach me something about being interrogated.

"Obviously, your father isn't here," he says, walking around me, his arm brushing against my shoulder. "But he is waiting for you at another location. I just need to ask you a few questions before I take you to him." He's behind me and so close the heat of his breath is on my neck. "Let me start off by introducing myself. I'm Knox Savage."

Knox Savage? Where have I heard that name before?

He lets out a gruff chuckle and his breath tickles the hairs on my neck, sending a chill through me. "You don't know me, so don't bother sifting through those pretty little thoughts."

"Pretty thoughts?"

Crap! One-word answers, Becky! Don't let him get to you.

He rounds me so I can see him, but he faces away from me as he pretends to look around the empty garage. I get a strange urge to bite the back of his strong neck, which only makes me think of August. Who knows what he's up to? Probably sitting in the café writing about the advantages of wool socks over cotton. Maybe he's in his apartment right now, having his wool socks slowly pulled off by some trust-fund hussy.

August lives in his perfect bachelor pad on the lower east side. He can flip his blonde hair back while sipping a cappuccino in a dusky coffee shop and no one will judge him because he's surrounded by hipsters. Tapping away at his keyboard, he writes about vintage sweaters and suede oxfords for his highly successful men's fashion blog. I, on the other hand, live in a quaint—code word for *crappy*—studio apartment in midtown—okay, Hell's Kitchen—where I can occasionally gorge on Doritos while watching CSI without August's judgment.

Knox turns around slowly and fixes me with that steely glare that once again halts my breath. "Here's the deal, Rebecca."

He pauses when he sees my eyes narrow. No one has called me Rebecca in years. When I left Bensonhurst, I became Becky. Someone sweet and innocent and, yes, maybe even a bit naïve. The fact that he called me Rebecca tells me this guy truly is here on my father's behalf. Suddenly, I feel sick to my stomach. This is serious.

His glare softens as he reaches for my arms. "You look pale."

My fingers are tingling. I'm going to pass out. I take a few quick breaths to rush some oxygen to my brain. Within seconds, the tingling goes away.

"Shit," I whisper.

He lets go of my arms and his eyes harden. "As I was saying, here's what you're going to do, Rebecca. You're going to go home right now and pretend as if this never happened. Come Monday morning, you will walk to work with your preppy boyfriend and pretend as if this never happened. You'll sit down at your desk in the evidence locker and, again, you'll pretend as if none of this ever happened… until you receive a phone call at precisely 8:12 a.m. Then you will do everything that is asked of you. You will follow every instruction to the letter. Is that clear?"

Every morning, August greets me at my front door with a skinny latte and a kiss. Then he walks me to work while we catch up on the previous day's news. After that, he takes the subway to his lower east side sanctuary and the cycle repeats. Sometimes he'll show up at my apartment early, so he can make love to me before work. Come to think of it, we never really see each other in the evening anymore.

I stare into Knox's cold blue eyes and now I'm ready to let him have it. "Okay, *Knox*. I think you have me mistaken for someone else. Someone who capitulates to my father's every whim. I'm not afraid of my father."

He breaks into a smile again when I say this. He doesn't believe that for a second.

"I'm not afraid of him!" I insist, sounding like a petulant child. I might as well start jumping up and down and plugging my ears with my fingers. "I'm not helping you or my father. Now please take me home. I have to rest for work tomorrow."

"I can't take you home until you agree to my terms."

"And if I refuse to agree to your terms?"

He looks into my eyes, one of his eyebrows cocked, daring me to follow through on this threat. "Then you'll never go home."

I don't question this. I don't protest. Because I can see it in his eyes. He's serious. He'll keep me here as long as it takes.

5

"WELL, YOU CAN'T hide me here forever. You obviously need something from me. Something time-sensitive or you could have sent me a handwritten letter via pony express. So I think I'll just wait it out."

He laughs, a hearty sexy laugh, even throwing his head back. God, he's way too sexy for words. The more he laughs, the more uncomfortable I become. He's one step ahead of me. And something tells me he always will be.

"Your disappearance will only lend credence to your father's cause. And it will be most advantageous to my mission. So you can stall all you want. It won't make your situation any easier."

This is where I crap my pants. Not literally, but almost. I have to get some leverage in this situation.

"What do I get if I cooperate? Besides my freedom."

He reaches up and brushes his thumb across the corner of his mouth as he smiles. It's an incredibly sexy gesture. As if I've just asked him an embarrassing question. But I haven't. He's just amused. Amused with my naiveté.

"You're not really in a position to negotiate."

"Then how do I get in that position?" I cover my mouth when I realize what I've said and he lets out another heart laugh. "That's not what I meant!"

My face is burning hot with embarrassment, but he just continues to chuckle.

"Your dad told me you might be a tough sell. But there's no one who can't be bought."

He reaches for my hair and I bat his hand away. "Don't touch me."

He smiles at my defiance. "Interesting hair color. Matches your eyes… I guess."

I glance down at my shoulder where my brown hair flows down over my coral silk tank top. "What's so interesting about it?"

He shakes his head and turns away from me. For a moment, I get a strong feeling Knox knows me. Does he know my real hair color? No, that's ridiculous. He's too young to be one of the goons who worked for my father four years ago.

"Have you ever heard the name Frank Mainella?"

He's still facing away from me, walking toward the

corner as he asks this question. I'm surprised he doesn't want to look me in the eye, to gauge my reaction. He strikes me as the kind of guy who would want to see my eyes widen and my body trembling at the mere mention of a name.

"I don't know who that is."

"Don't lie to me, Rebecca."

"Why do you keep calling me Rebecca? My name is Becky!"

He turns on his heel and glares at me. "Don't lie to me, Rebecca! Do you know Frank Mainella?"

The trembling in my hands intensifies as he strides toward me. "I don't know anyone named Frank!"

He grabs me by the arms and his face is inches from mine as he roars, "What do you know about Frank Mainella?"

"Let me go!"

My struggling only makes him tighten his grip. "Tell me what you saw and I'll let you go!"

My heart is pounding as his fingers dig into my biceps. But my gaze keeps falling to his lips. Those lips.

"Stop it. You're hurting me." I murmur these words and he loosens his grip on me just slightly. "Please," I beg, my chest heaving, not sure what I'm begging for.

His eyes soften into a mesmerizing sky-blue. The kind of sky you could lie back and get lost in for hours. And suddenly I'm lost in a memory.

6

eight years ago

I'm fifteen years old and lying on my bed doing my homework. The doorbell rings and, as usual, I wait for my mom to answer it. A couple of minutes later, the ding-dong of the doorbell comes again. And again I wait.

On the third ring, I resign myself to the fact that I'm going to have to leave my room and possibly face my father. He won't answer the door; not even if he's sitting in the recliner right next to it. It's not because he's lazy or chauvinistic. It's a security measure.

Security. As if anyone could ever feel secure around my father knowing the things he's done.

I race down the steps and I'm relieved to find the living room empty. I shoot toward the front door and glance through the peephole. What is Marco doing here?

Technically, I'm not allowed to answer the door when I'm home alone. But this isn't a stranger. My dad loves Marco Leone like a son.

I sigh as I pull the door open. Marco's blue eyes quickly glance over my body before he speaks. "Your dad here?"

"No. He's probably down at the shop."

My dad owns Veneto's on 9th Street, but no one ever calls it a restaurant. It's *the shop*. Because there's a lot more going on there than food.

Marco glances over his shoulder nervously. "Can I come in and wait for him?"

"He might not be home for hours." He looks anxious, but it's the desperate plea in his eyes that gets me. "Come in."

I've seen Marco around the neighborhood for years, but I haven't seen him around much since his mother was killed two years ago. His father left when he was a kid. So when his mom died, there wasn't anything tying him to Bensonhurst. He must be twenty now if he was eighteen then.

"Have a seat," I say, motioning to the sofa. "You want something to drink."

My heart is pounding as I realize I'm alone in my house with a guy who's five years older than me. My father would probably kill me if he knew I answered the door while I was home alone.

Marco shakes his head as he sits back on the brown leather sofa. "I'm not thirsty. I'll just wait here."

I sit a couple of feet away from him. The sofa exhales a puff of air that smells like cigar smoke. I pull both my legs up and face Marco as I sit cross-legged.

"You haven't been around much since…."

He stares at the floor in front of his feet. "I've been busy."

"Doing what?"

Some would call me nosy. My father would call me inquisitive.

Even after my father discovered I saw what he did to Uncle Frank, he still refers to me as his inquisitive, perfect princess. My father knows I'd never tell a soul what I saw. But that doesn't mean I still feel the same way about my father. He's no longer the hero of the neighborhood to me. When I look at him now, I see a two-faced thug.

There's something magnetic about Marco. Just sitting there with one arm draped over the side of the sofa, looking around so he doesn't have to look at me. There's an intense energy pulsing off of him. Pulling me toward him.

Without realizing it, I've reached my hand out to touch the tattoo on his forearm. His skin is so warm and stretched taut over his firm muscles.

"What are you doing?"

I look up from the tattoo of his mother's name—

Ella—and he almost looks angry.

"I'm sorry." I pull my hand away. "I didn't meant to do that."

He stares at me for a moment before his gaze falls to my lips. He shakes his head and looks away. Am I giving off that same energy?

I clasp my hands in my lap so I don't accidentally touch him again. "So what have you been up to?"

"I've been in prison."

His voice is hard and I know he's telling the truth. One thing I've learned from being part of the family is that you don't ask people about their crimes. There's a paranoia about wires that runs thick through this community. Asking someone for specifics about a crime they've committed is like wearing a sign that reads, *I'm a rat.*

But I can't help myself.

"What did you do?"

He glances sideways at me and a tiny smile curls the left side of his mouth. "Nothing."

"How long were you in prison for doing nothing?"

He chuckles and it's such a sexy sound, my arms sprout goosebumps. "Nineteen months."

"You must have done a whole lot of nothing to serve nineteen months."

He turns to me and his smile is gone. "Listen, Rebecca, you can't tell anyone you saw me here. You understand? After I see your dad, I'm leaving Bensonhurst for good."

"Why?"

"Because there's nothing left for me here."

A sharp pain sparks inside my chest. "You're never coming back?"

He shakes his head and once again his gaze falls on my lips. "Nah. I've got some business to take care of."

My heart thumps in every inch of my skin as I stare at his lips. It would be so wrong for me to kiss him. But it's all I want to do. If this is the last time I'm ever going to see him, there's no harm in just a kiss. Right?

"When did you get out of prison?"

"This morning."

He got out this morning. That means he hasn't kissed a girl in at least nineteen months. No wonder he keeps staring at my lips.

Suddenly, I'm in his lap, my hands clutching his face, my mouth on his. We're both breathing so heavily I can hear the air whooshing inside our mouths.

"Stop," he insists as his hands slide over my hips. "We can't do this."

"Why not? I'm not a virgin."

It's a lie, but when am I going to have an opportunity like this? After today, I'll never see him again. Then I'll always wonder about that energy.

He grabs my face and forces my head back so he can look me in the eye. "You're fifteen and you're not a virgin?" He looks appalled. "Who was it? Who the fuck did it? Tell me and I'll fucking kill him."

I can't help but smile at this reaction. For a moment, I consider making up a name. But I can see from the fierce glare in his eyes, that he would probably hunt down this fictional guy and tear out his eyes.

"Okay, fine. I'm still a virgin." He easily lifts me off his lap and sets me down on the sofa next to him. "But I don't want to be a virgin anymore."

He shakes his head as he stands front the sofa. "I can't stay here."

"Why?"

"Because you're fifteen years old and I don't want your dad to murder me. Like I said, I've got shit to take care of. And I need to be alive to do that."

He heads for the door and I follow after him. "But I thought you had to see my dad."

He looks me in the eye as he thinks. "Just tell him I came by and I'll get in touch with him soon. But only tell *him*. Don't tell anyone else. Understood?"

I nod, pressing my lips together to try to hold back the tears of rejection. He lets go of the door handle and turns to me. He takes my face in his strong hands and forces me to look at him.

"Don't just give yourself to any asshole who'll have you. You're too beautiful for that. Promise me you'll wait."

I nod again as the first tear rolls down my cheek and

he leans in to kiss me. This is not the hungry kiss we shared a couple of minutes ago. This is a slow, tender kiss; the kind that will be burned into my memory forever. He pulls away and lays a soft kiss on my forehead.

"Tampering with evidence in a federal investigation," he whispers with that crooked smile that makes the dimple in his chin more pronounced.

Then he kisses my cheekbone and walks out of my life forever.

7

"MARCO?"

There's a flash of recognition in his eyes, but it's gone in an instant. "That's not my name." His mouth is set in a hard line as he tightens his grip on my arms again. "What do you know about Frank?"

We're so close, my chest is pressed against his. I should knee him in the crotch, but I have nowhere to run to. And I'm losing my resolve. I should never have walked Lita to the train today.

Who am I kidding?

If they hadn't found me on 42nd Street, they would have found me in my apartment. Knox works for my father. And if Knox is really Marco—I think I'd recognize those blue eyes anywhere—then he's been working for my father since before he was sent to prison for tampering with evidence. Ten years can do a lot to a man in this line of business.

"Tell me who you are—who you *really* are—and I'll tell you about Frank."

He loosens his grasp and shakes his head. "You think this is a game? I've already told you, you're in no position to negotiate." He smiles and tilts his head. "And you know that."

The heat of his breath on my nose makes my heart race. I can't outtalk him or outsmart him. But maybe… maybe I can outrun him.

"Okay. I'll go to work tomorrow and do whatever you want me to do. Can I go now?"

"No." He finally lets go of my arms. "You're going to sit down and tell me everything you know about Frank Mainella. Then you can do whatever I want you to do."

He points at a stack of three tires for me to sit down. I sigh as I walk over, pulling up my skirt so I don't get tire dust or grease on it, and take a seat. The hard rubber is cool against the backs of my bare legs.

"Tell me what this is all about." He glares at me, angry that I'm still making demands. "Please," I plead softly. "Is my father in trouble?"

His chiseled features soften. "Yes. Your dad's in a lot of trouble. He's being arraigned tomorrow afternoon for the murder of Frank Mainella."

I cover my face with my hands and will myself not to cry. This is what I wanted, isn't it?

"I need to know everything you know about Frank Mainella's death, and the weeks leading up to it. Can you do that?"

His voice is softer now, as if "angry Knox Savage" was just a role he was playing. I draw in a deep breath and look up. His eyes are pleading with me to cooperate. He doesn't want to keep me here any more than I want to be here.

"I saw him do it." I suck in another shaky breath. "My father killed him, in our living room, ten years ago."

He kneels before me and looks up into my eyes. "Rebecca, you have to tell me everything you saw."

That look. Those eyes. The way he lays his hand on my knee. That's all it takes for me to tell him everything. Because that's what my father wants. Isn't it?

His hand slides off my knee and I nearly gasp at the way his touch feels so electric. Not at all clumsy the way August's touch often feels.

He stands and offers his hand to help me up. "I'll drive you home."

"That's it?" I ask, taking his hand.

He pulls me up and my body feels as exhausted as my mind. It must be close to midnight. But, suddenly, I'm not ready to leave.

"No, that's not it. Tomorrow the hard part begins."

8

KNOX'S GOONS LOOK reluctant when he tells them he'll be driving me home himself. But they know better than to argue with him. We walk silently through another corridor then exit the garage through a back door. The alley is dark, but the moonlight glistens on the silver sports car.

"I'm taking you home myself so I can check your home for bugs. So, when we enter your apartment, don't say anything until I give you the all clear signal."

He presses the key fob to unlock the car then opens the passenger door for me.

"What's the all clear signal?"

I slide into the passenger seat and he pauses to watch me pull on my seatbelt. "I'll let you know when it's all clear."

The hum of the engine tells me this is one powerful ride. Powerful and silent. We slip unnoticed through the streets of Manhattan. I'm surprised I wasn't blindfolded again. Now I can see that we were in a garage in Harlem.

There are so many questions I want to ask him as we drive toward midtown. Mainly, I want to know if this sexy, self-possessed man is Marco. His face only looks like Marco in the sharp edges of his chiseled cheekbones. And his eyes. I'm certain I'd recognize those eyes anywhere. But his nose is different; a bit broader. And the dimple in his chin is gone.

We arrive at my building while I'm still contemplating his face. He pulls his expensive car into a guest space in the underground parking lot. Then he grabs my hand before I can exit the car.

"Remember: Don't say a word. There could be bugs everywhere. Even in the elevator. Got it?"

I nod, already practicing my tight-lipped act. Eager to please this complete stranger. He smiles as if he can hear my thoughts.

We ride the elevator up to the fourth floor. He follows closely behind me as I lead him to my door. Before I can turn the key in the lock, he places his hand over mine.

"I'll go in first."

He finishes turning the key, then hands it over to me. I take a step back as he turns the knob and slowly pushes the door open.

The apartment is pitch black, just the way I like it.

"The light switch is—"

He shushes me and a swell of anger overcomes me. I didn't leave Bensonhurst four years ago only to get mixed up in another one of my dad's schemes. I'm about to tell him to leave my apartment, when he turns around. He's smiling as he points at the light switch on the wall. That smile is so disarming. I nod and he flips the switch.

She presses a finger to his lips to indicate the need for silence, then he continues into my apartment. I grab a couple of glasses of ice water while he searches the kitchen and the bathroom. When he moves toward the living-slash-sleeping area, I follow him.

My stomach is clenched tightly as he sifts through my closet and my dresser. When he reaches for the top drawer of my nightstand, I almost yell for him to stop. He slides the drawer open and pauses as he stares at the contents. Then he reaches into the drawer and pulls out a very large vibrator and a box of ribbed condoms.

"Please put those back."

He shushes me again as he opens the box of condoms. Does he really think he's going to find a listening device in there? Then he pulls out a strip of condoms. He dangles the strip from his fingers, eyeing it curiously. Then he tosses the condoms onto the bed and places the empty box and the vibrator back in the drawer.

He rounds the bed and my heart races as he makes his

way toward me. Stopping right in front of me, he leans in until his lips are on my ear.

"All clear."

A shiver travels over my neck and shoulders as he wraps his lips around my earlobe. His breath is hot in my ear. I don't know if I want this. All I know is that I don't want him to stop.

"Is that the signal?" I ask breathily.

His hand is firm as he clasps the back of my head, tilting my head to the side so he can kiss my neck. His other hand slides around my waist and down to my butt. He pulls my hips against his so his erection is stiff against my thigh. *That* must be the signal. A very *huge* signal.

Oh, God. Am I really going to do this? Am I going to cheat on August with a guy I met hours ago? When I'm *sober?*

As he gathers up the back of my skirt and slides his firm hand into my panties, I know the answer to that is yes. A very *huge* yes.

9

I RAISE MY hands so I can unknot his tie. But he grabs my hands and glares at me.

"I'll do that," he says, pushing my hands down near his crotch.

"But, I want to do it."

I flash him my sexiest come-hither smile and he shakes his head.

"You're not going to do anything," he growls. "You're going to lie back and pay attention as I show you what it means to be fucked, in every sense of the word. And when I'm done, you're going to have only one choice: To do everything I ask of you. Understood?"

Holy shit. What have I gotten myself into?

Something so completely screwed up that I know

there's no way out. I'm falling further into this rabbit hole by the second. Gleefully falling in after Knox. Hoping he'll soften the impact when I hit the bottom.

"Understood," I whisper.

Then his mouth is on mine. The moment I've been waiting for. And it's as perfect, and electric, as I imagined it would be. The way he kisses me, fast and then slow, hard and then tender, I know there's no turning back. Because there's no way he can deny it now.

This is Marco.

Once he's kissed me long enough for me to relinquish all control, he steps back. "Take off your panties."

I slip out of my panties and kick them a few feet away. He steps forward and slides his hand between my thighs. His finger quickly finds my clit and my knees instantly begin to buckle. He wraps his thick arm around my waist to steady me, caressing me slowly as my limbs grow weaker.

Then, suddenly, he jams two fingers inside me and I gasp. "Oh, my God."

He slides his fingers out of me and my moisture gushes out at the same time. He rubs my clit again, firmer this time, until I can't breathe. He tightens his arm around my waist and lifts me off the floor. Then he sits me down on the edge of the bed. I begin to lie back and he shakes his head.

He kneels before me, slowly pulling off his tie, then

his coat and shirt. Spreading my knees slowly, he lifts my skirt to look at me. I can feel my cheeks getting hot. He lowers his head between my legs and I dig my nails into his muscular back as he devours me.

His tongue massages my hard nub until I'm certain my juices have soaked through the comforter and the sheets beneath it. My body trembling, his back screaming with red scratch marks, he finally comes up for air. The thirst in his eyes is not even close to being sated. He doesn't just want more. He *needs* more.

"Take off your clothes and lie down on your belly."

I do as he says and, when I lie down, I notice the strip of condoms. The mattress shifts under his weight as he slides my legs apart and climbs on behind me. The skin of his leg rubs against the inside of my thigh. He takes my hands and pulls them behind my back. Then the smooth silk fabric of his tie is cool against my skin as he loops it around my wrists. He pulls the knot tight and lets out a soft chuckle.

"You've never been on the wrong side of the law, Rebecca." He lies down on top of me, his weight pressing me into the mattress as his erection rubs against the crease of my cheeks. "I'm going to teach you a little lesson about having your freedom taken away, so you can know just how serious I am about this job."

His hand slides beneath me to cup my breast. Then he lifts my hips and the tip of his erection is at the entrance of my vagina.

"Wait! Aren't you going to put on one of those?"

"Is that what you want?"

"Yes."

"Then, no. I'm not."

"Wait, wait, wait! No! I mean, *no*. That's *not* what I want." Shut up, Rebecca. He's not going to fall for your stupid attempt to salvage this last shred of control.

He laughs again, but this time his laugh sounds a little insane. "Rebecca, I'm not going to impregnate you. I'm incapable of such things."

I let out a deep sigh. "Please just tell me who you are."

"How does it feel to be in this position? Physically surrendered." He slides his cock inside me and I cry out. "Mentally surrendered. Incapable of getting the answers you so desperately need."

He slides out of me and suddenly I feel hollow. Incomplete. He places the tip of his cock against my opening again and I hold my breath.

"Please."

"Please, what?"

"Please put it in," I beg.

He teases me a bit, sliding in just an inch or two. Then he rams into me, filling me completely and my chest trembles with desperation.

"More," I beg. "Faster. Harder."

He thrusts into me, using my wetness to pierce me

deeper with each stroke. My arms and neck are getting tired from this position, with the side of my face pressed against the mattress. As if he can sense this, he pulls his cock out of me and presses my ass down so I'm lying flat.

He straightens my right leg then bends my left leg as he enters me from behind. At this angle, with his chest pressed firmly against my back, I begin to lose myself quickly.

The hot friction of our bodies makes our bodies slick with sweat. His cock fills me, stretches me, stabs me. His mouth devours my neck as his hand massages my breast, pinching my nipple so I can feel that carnal pull in my lower abdomen. He moves in and out of me, panting heavily into my ear as his hand slips between my thighs.

"Oh, Knox!" I cry, my body convulsing.

My thighs tremble as his thrusting speeds up. He growls, a low primal roar as he bites down on my neck and explodes inside me. He holds his finger over my clit, softly caressing me as my muscles contract and release. Until I come undone.

We lie breathless, boneless as we recover. Then he slowly reaches between us and unties me. He tosses the tie to the floor and I sigh as I stretch my arms. Then a sick feeling develops in my stomach as an equally sick thought materializes in my mind.

I don't want to be free.

10

I WAKE TO find the other side of the bed empty. For a moment, I consider I may have dreamed the entire ordeal with Knox. Maybe I even dreamed the part where I was taken to the garage.

Then I see his tie strewn across the beige carpet next to the strip of condoms. And I hear the shower going. It was real. Knox is real.

Or is he?

I leap out of bed. I have to find out if Knox is Marco and this is probably the only opportunity I'll have to do so. I scramble around the bed until I see his slacks tossed onto the armchair a few feet away from my bed. I dig into the pockets and find his wallet. When I open it, I'm not surprised to find no identification. All I see is a black credit card bearing the name Knox Savage.

"You're out of towels."

I drop the wallet and slacks onto the armchair and spin around. Knox is standing in the doorway of the bathroom completely naked. Water drips from the glistening black hair on his head and his muscular body, all over the floor, forming small puddles around his feet. My eyes flit to his forearm, scanning his skin for the tattoo of Marco's mother's name. His entire forearm is covered in a sleeve of tattoos.

"I'm sorry," I mutter. "I'll get you a towel."

I move toward the closet where I keep both my clothes and my linens, but he beats me there. His arms lock around my waist as he presses his naked body against my naked body.

"Find anything interesting in my wallet?"

His blue eyes look even bluer in the morning light. I want to scream at him. *Just tell me the truth!* But I don't want to know what kind of lesson he'll teach me after that. Or maybe I do want to know.

"Who are you?" I shout. "Tell me who you are?"

"Are you making demands of me, Rebecca?" He grabs my face, his thumb and fingertips digging into my cheeks. When I don't answer, he pulls my face to his so our noses are touching and roars. "Are you making demands of me?"

I don't say anything. I couldn't speak if I tried. My throat has closed and my mouth is dry. If he doesn't kill me now, he will do it eventually.

He crushes his lips to mine and I fight to breathe as he ravages my mouth. One of his hands grasps my ass, pulling me against him, as his other hand finds my clit. His fingers glide right past my pleasure spot as he thrusts them inside me. He curls his fingers, massaging and searching until he finds my g-spot and I begin to crumble.

"Please stop," I plead. It feels so good it's almost painful. I don't know if I can take it.

His thumb massages my clit as his middle finger caresses my g-spot and I shake my head adamantly.

"Please."

"Please, what?" he murmurs against my lips.

"This is too much. Please… just fuck me."

He chuckles as he removes his hand from between my legs and proceeds to get dressed.

"What are you doing?" I ask incredulously.

He ignores me as he continues to pull on his clothes over his still damp body. He wraps his tie around his fist and musses up his hair as he walks toward the door.

When he reaches the door, he turns around and points at me with the same finger he just used to torture me. "Don't ever fucking spy on me again or this is going to end very badly."

He unlocks the door and pauses for a moment. "Now take a shower and make yourself pretty. You have work to do." He reaches for the doorknob then pauses again, my heart pounding as I anticipate what he's going to say or do next.

He looks into my eyes as he slowly slides his finger into his mouth and smiles. "Be a good girl at work today and I'll finish you tonight."

That's all he needed to say. A promise. *There will be more, if you behave.*

11

I SCRUB MYSELF in the shower, but I can't seem to rid myself of Knox's scent. I don't think there's any of him left on me, but I can still smell him. As if he's embedded so deeply inside me, in places I can't reach.

August will be here to walk me to work in less than an hour. I have to hurry up and get dressed and blow dry my hair. I have to make it seem as though nothing has happened. Then I can spring it on August when we get to the precinct.

August, it's over. I've found a guy who can fuck my brains out. Literally. I think I've lost my mind in a matter of hours, but I've never felt better.

The doorbell rings as I'm pulling my bra out of the dresser. *Shit!* He must be here early hoping to get in a quick fuck before work. I glance down at myself. I'm wearing a towel wrapped around my body and another towel around my head.

The doorbell sounds again. I slam my dresser drawer shut and scramble for the door. I fumble with the lock for a moment, wondering if Knox left traces of me on the lock and the doorknob when he left. Pulling the door open, I'm not prepared to feel utterly disgusted when I see August's smiling face.

I want to slap him and ask him why I haven't been invited to his apartment in four months. I want to accuse him of cheating on me. I want to shake him so hard the truth falls out of him like loose change.

Instead, I smile and invite him inside. He leans in to kiss me as he steps over the threshold and I allow it. In my head all I can think is, *You bastard. You lying little geek.*

"Good morning, sunshine."

He immediately walks into the kitchen area and begins putting on a pot of coffee. It's something I usually find endearing. How he knows and supports my caffeine addiction. Today I find it annoying.

"How did you sleep?" he asks as he fills the coffee pot with water then pours the water into the coffee machine.

"I slept great. Like a baby."

"Really? Did you fill that prescription the doctor gave you?"

I open the dresser drawer again. "Nope. I was just

really exhausted."

"Really? What did you do last night?"

He runs his fingers through his soft blonde hair as he walks toward me wearing a sly grin. The grin that says, *I'm smarter, richer, and better looking than you, and I know it*. And suddenly I'm reminded of the day I met August.

Lita had taken me to a dinner party at her then-boyfriend's house in the Hamptons. Her boyfriend, Marty, was some hot-shot in-house lawyer for a huge record label. August was at the party with a date, though I didn't find this out until forty minutes into our conversation when his date stumbled out onto the patio and tried to punch me in the face.

I should have known then not to trust August. But he was so charming. And *so* well-dressed. The man dressed better than I did. And the fact that he dumped his date right there was equally impressive. He was sleeping at my apartment, making me coffee, and calling me *honey* less than two weeks later.

Yes, I fall for the worst guys. Even now, as August casts that sly smile in my direction, my stomach does a backflip. He reaches for me and my towel falls as I back up into the dresser.

He chuckles as his gaze slides over my naked body. "God, you are so beautiful."

He grabs my hips and pulls me toward him. His hands are soft. The hands of someone who drinks coffee and types on his laptop all day long. But they're also strong as he holds me against him.

He leans in to kiss me and I turn my head. "Stop."

"Why?" he murmurs as he kisses my neck. "You taste so good."

"August, stop!" I push him hard in the chest.

"What's wrong? Are you on your period?"

"Ugh! No, I am *not* on my period! You're... you're *cheating* on me, aren't you?"

His entire face scrunches up in confusion. "What? What are you talking about?"

He moves toward me and I hold my hand out to stop him. "Why haven't I been to your apartment in four months?"

He chuckles. "You think I'm cheating on you because you hate coming to my apartment. Honey, I stopped inviting you after you turned me down six times in a row."

"You are so predictable, August! I knew you would say something like that."

His smile disappears. If there's one thing August hates, it's being called predictable or unoriginal. His entire life is designed around his ability to bring together the old and the new, the fresh and the vintage, and make it into something effortlessly classic.

He tempers his inner disappointment as he takes a step back. "Becky, I love you. You know I would never do anything to jeopardize that love. What we have is solid.

It's… everlasting. Please don't let this… this paranoia destroy us."

"Paranoia?"

"Well, what else would you call it? You accuse me of cheating on you with absolutely no evidence other than the fact that I haven't invited you to my apartment lately."

"So I'm paranoid?"

"Becky, please."

"Stop calling me Becky!"

"What?"

I shake my head as I turn around and grab the TV remote off the top of the dresser. I turn on the TV and it's already on the correct channel. I watch the local morning show every morning before work. It helps me think. It keeps me focused as I get dressed and ready for work. Otherwise, I get distracted. I know that when the weather girl comes on for the second time, it's time for me to get my ass out the door or I'll be late for work.

The weather girl is telling us what a beautiful summer day it's going to be in Manhattan. I set the remote back on top of the dresser and pull my bra out of the top drawer. August sneaks up behind me, pressing his lips to my ear.

"Let me make it up to you. We can spend the night at my house tonight. It's Friday. We can spend the whole weekend there." His tongue traces the outer edge of my ear and I close my eyes, trying to block out thoughts of Knox. "I'll make you breakfast in bed and then I'll feast on you."

The weather girl disappears and a breaking news alert comes on.

"Breaking news. John Veneto, the suspected boss of the brutal Veneto Crime Family, is being arraigned this afternoon for the murder of Frank Mainella. Frank Mainella was murdered ten years ago, but his body was never found until three weeks ago when a construction company began demolition on an old Bensonhurst strip mall and found Mainella's remains encased in concrete below a printing shop. The Veneto Crime Family has controlled Bensonhurst and surrounding neighborhoods for more than thirty years. Police are optimistic that this arrest will restore order to this flourishing neighborhood."

"Veneto?" August repeats my last name aloud. "I didn't think that was a common last name."

"It's not."

August follows me as I move to the closet to get some clothes. "Aren't you from Bensonhurst?"

"He's my father, okay? Are you happy now? Want to go write about it on your *fucking* blog?"

He chuckles again as he leans in to kiss my neck again. "That's kind of hot."

Without thinking, I bend my arm to my chest then I elbow him in the ribs. "Get out of my apartment, August. We're over!"

12

I TRY NOT to cry as I walk to the midtown station on 35th. Instead, I apply my makeup while walking through the crowds on the sidewalk. Ignoring the angry complaints for me to watch where I'm going. I swipe some lipstick over my mouth and tuck my compact into my purse.

Stopping on the sidewalk, I look up at the building I've worked in for thirteen months. It looks different.

The brown brick and gold clad siding look even gaudier than usual. A boxy design that used to symbolize strength now looks ridiculous and outdated. This department is no match for men like Knox Savage. As long as he can get to someone inside. Someone as weak and susceptible as me.

For all I know, Knox probably orchestrated this whole

mess with August. All so he could find me last night on 42nd Street at my most vulnerable moment. As if he were rescuing me.

No, that's just insane. Why would anyone go to such lengths to make another person feel insecure? Just to mess with their head. Then again, I know next to nothing about Knox other than the fact that he works for my father.

I enter the station and say my good mornings to the officers manning the front desk. *You shouldn't be so nice to me. I'm going to betray you in a few hours,* I almost blurt out. I take the elevator down to the sub-level. The doors open and Detective Charlie Hunter is standing in the concrete corridor.

"Good morning, Veneto," he says in his smooth jazz voice.

Charlie Hunter is the one mistake I made in the entire department. Everyone here knows who my father is. Some people think it's funny to joke about it. *Did you see your dad this weekend? Help your dad bury any dead bodies this weekend?*

Charlie was the only one in this testosterone and coffee-fueled group of grown men who seemed normal. So I thought I'd be friendly. We went for drinks at a steakhouse around the corner. I didn't think it was a date. Charlie disagreed. When he found out I was seeing someone, he dug up a bunch of dirt on August and left it in a manila folder on my desk in the evidence locker.

As soon as I realized what it was, I shredded the folder

and all its contents. I didn't want to read it. Though, I must admit I regret that a little. Especially considering everything that's happened with August.

"Hey, Charlie," I say, stepping out of the elevator.

He stops on the threshold of the elevator and watches me. "Hey, tough luck about your dad."

I don't have to turn around. I can hear the smug grin in his voice.

"Fuck off, Charlie."

13

TELLING A DETECTIVE to fuck off was probably not my smartest move. But I'm too on edge to deal with smug assholes. I sit at my desk in the evidence locker, staring at the phone, willing it to ring so we can get this over with.

"You all right, Veneto? You look like you're gonna puke."

Tracy Warner is my coworker and the only person in this precinct I can be honest with. Until today, that is. I can't tell her anything about Knox or my father or Frank Mainella.

"It's this whole thing with my dad. I'm sick about it. And everyone's looking at me weird. This... this is the last place I want to be right now."

It's not a total lie.

"You want to take the day off? I'll tell the sergeant you got violently ill and puked all over an evidence bag."

"Way to get me fired."

She smiles and her brown skin crinkles around her eyes. "Honey, you look like shit. Weren't you the one who told me your father was dead to you?"

I shrug. "Yeah, that was when I knew I could go hug him any time I wanted to."

Did I just say that out loud?

"Girl, there ain't nothing wrong with loving your screwed up family," she says, rubbing my back. "I told you about my cousin Evan. That boy been in and out of jail more times than I can count and I still pick him up every time he's released. It's blood, baby. Ain't nothin' stronger."

Blood. I wonder what kind of evidence they have against my father. What evidence I have to destroy? It can't be blood. I saw Frank Mainella die. There was no blood. My father unplugged the downstairs lamp and tightened the cord around Frank's neck. Then he held it until Frank's eyes turned bloodshot and his tongue lolled to the side.

The phone rings and my heart leaps into my throat.

"You want me to get that?" Tracy says, leaning over me as she reaches for the phone.

"No!" I say, my hand beating hers to the handset.

I pick up the phone and press it to my ear so I don't have to see Tracy's reaction. "Hello? Um, I mean,

Midtown South. Veneto speaking. May I help you?"

"Veneto, this is Savage." His voice is beautiful. "Rebecca, are you there?"

"Yes! Yes, I'm here. How may I help you?"

"Rebecca, I need you to check your email. Your private email address. There's a message for you from Knox Security. Follow the instructions in that email. Good luck."

He hangs up before I can ask him if I'll be seeing him tonight. I'm behaving like a desperate schoolgirl, hoping for just one more glance from the hot captain of the football team. I sigh as I open up the browser on my computer. Then I stop myself. I can't check it on my work computer.

I pull my phone out of my purse and open the email app. Sure enough, the most recent email is from Knox Security. When I open it up, the logo looks very familiar. There's an attachment, but it requires a password.

I enter the name Frank Mainella and nothing happens. I enter my father's name and nothing. It has to be Rebecca. I enter my name and *still* nothing happens.

Then it hits me.

I enter the password I use for all my personal accounts. The password I think no one but me knows. Immediately a video message opens. I pause the video and excuse myself to the restroom so I can watch it. I take a seat on the toilet and press play.

His voice sends a chill through me. He gives me clear instructions on the location and catalog number of the file I need to get my hands on. It's not in this precinct. It's in the Queens forensics lab. I'm not surprised. We hold very little evidence here in Midtown South.

Knox goes on explaining an elaborate lie, which I'm supposed to memorize so I can gain access to the evidence. He signs off with a nod of his head. I'm almost saddened that there was no promise of seeing each other tonight. But of course he can't put that on video.

"Who was it?" Tracy asks as I sit at my desk in front of her.

"Who was what?"

"On the phone, before you went to the restroom?"

"Oh. Oh *that*. That was just Charlie asking if he can take me out for a drink to drown my sorrows."

"He just won't let it go, will he?"

I tuck my phone into my purse and lay my head on my desk. "I'm really not feeling well. Maybe it's not just this mess with my dad."

"Honey, you go on home. I've got this."

"Thanks, Tracy." I give her a one-armed hug before I leave the locker.

I leave through a different entrance than I entered, so I don't have to hear any more comments about my father. But I still manage to run into Charlie again on the sidewalk.

"Leaving so soon?" he says. "Is the pressure finally getting to you? You look a little pale."

I ignore him as I walk past, then I stop. I can't let this guy bully me. If he can't deal with rejection, let's see how he deals with wrath.

I turn on my heel to face him. "You know what, Charlie, you're pathetic. You think digging up dirt on my boyfriend is going to make me want to date you instead? You think dragging my name through the mud then rubbing my face in it is going to make me respect you? You're nothing but a piece of shit who can't take rejection. Now leave me the hell alone before I file a harassment claim."

He stares at me for a moment as he drops his cigarette onto the concrete and stamps it out with his wingtip. "Where are you off to, Veneto? Awfully early to be leaving work."

"I'm going home to puke in my own toilet, while my boyfriend holds my hair back and screws me from behind. Have a nice day."

14

I TAKE A cab to Queens, but I ask the driver to drop me off a couple of blocks away—as Knox instructed me to. He doesn't want anyone, not even the cab driver, to know where I'm going. He didn't say it, but I also think this is so he can follow me. As I walk down Jamaica Avenue, I can almost sense Knox out there, watching my every move. And it makes me feel safe.

I enter the reception area and two uniformed police officers are manning the front counter. There's a chain link gate to their left bearing a large white sign bearing the words *Stop. Wait here until you are called.*

I approach the counter and the older officer comes up to greet me. "Can I help you?"

"Yes, I'm here from the 14th Precinct. Sergent Sullivan

sent me to pick up the…" I pause, just the way Knox told me to, "…the Sugarman case."

I hold out the badge that hangs around my neck. The officer with the gray hair and the hard, black eyes examines my badge. He buzzes me in and tells me how to get to another reception area where the clerk will pull the file for me.

You're probably wondering how I'm going to get away with this. I'm not.

I'm not actually going to do anything. When I get to the reception area, the clerk won't be there. She's going to be in the bathroom, violently ill from a little something someone put in her morning coffee. I'm going to get in there and take both the Sugarman file and the Veneto file. I will take the Sugarman file with me, but I'll stuff the Veneto file in the bottom drawer of the receptionist's desk. That's it.

It's a stall tactic. I'm not actually destroying evidence.

Without the evidence, there's no case against my father. As tempting as it is to destroy the file, that's not my job. And Knox made that very clear. We just need to buy some time.

And some freedom.

Without the file, the judge will most likely grant my father bail at today's arraignment. It will probably be an exorbitant amount, but Knox will take care of it. Then it's just a matter of waiting for me to be subpoenaed.

Knox didn't say what kind of evidence they found on Frank Mainella's skeletal remains, but it has to be something that ties Frank to our house in Bensonhurst. I can't think of any other reason they would need to subpoena me. But once I'm on the stand, that's when phase two of Operation Veneto Freedom begins.

Let me make this clear. I don't condone what my father did to Frank Mainella. In fact, I hate him for it. I suffered nightmares and anxiety for years after that night. But you can't help who you love. And I love my father despite the atrocities he's committed. I always will.

I stuff the Veneto file into the bottom drawer of the receptionist's desk and slide it closed. As I round the desk, I hear the sound of her heels clicking against the tile in the corridor. I go through the motions of requesting the Sugarman file. Her face is white as tissue paper as she drags herself back into the warehouse and retrieves the file for me. She hands it over and I thank her profusely. Then I suggest she get some rest. *There's a stomach bug going around.*

When I come out of the Crime Lab and step onto the sidewalk, I almost breathe a sigh of relief. Until I see Charlie standing on the sidewalk.

"Thought you were going home?"

"Are you following me?"

My heart is racing, but not with fury. This is bad. This is so, so bad. This was not part of the plan. The plan was for me to get in another cab a couple of blocks away. That cab was supposed to take me to my apartment where Knox would be waiting. One of his guys, disguised as a court courier, was supposed to deliver the file to the precinct. Then Knox Savage was going to *ravage* me.

"Why would I be following you?"

This is a trick question. Charlie's trying to get me to slip up and say something about my father.

"Because you're obsessed with me."

"You wish. I'm a fucking detective. It's my *job* to be here. Why are *you* here?"

"I work in evidence. It's my *job* to be here."

He rolls his eyes as he walks toward the entrance door. "Have fun getting fucked over a toilet."

Shit.

Shit, shit, shit, shit, shit!

This is *not* good. Charlie *cannot* know I was here.

I scurry down the sidewalk and flag down a cab. I shoot off the address for my apartment building, then I lean back to catch my breath. The cab comes to a screeching halt and my eyelids fly open. The cab door is wrenched open. I'm yanked out of the backseat by a guy in a suit and black sunglasses.

"Jesus Christ!" I yelp as he carries me to a black SUV, which is stopped in front of the cab.

"Shh!"

He stuffs me into the backseat and climbs in behind me. Then the car speeds away. Not in the direction of my apartment.

15

I WHIP MY head around to see who else is in the car with us. It's just me, the driver, the guy who threw me in here in the row of seats behind me, and Knox in the seat next to me. He's wearing a dark blue suit today. He's looking even more ravishing than last night. And he does not look happy.

I don't have to ask where we're going. It's obvious we're going back to the garage where this all began. I want to ask him how screwed we are, but I'm frightened of his response. Instead, we stare into each other's eyes for a while, his jaw clenching and unclenching.

I can't take this anymore.

"What are we going to do about Charlie?"

"You're not going to do anything. I'll take care of

Charlie."

"What do you mean by *take care of*? What are you going to do to him?"

"You worry about doing your job and I'll worry about mine."

"You can't hurt him. He's a prick, but he doesn't deserve to get hurt."

Knox leans forward suddenly and thrusts a pointed finger in my face. "You should have stuck to the fucking script! But, no, you had to go and antagonize that loser. Whatever happens to him now is *your* fault! It's on *your* head!"

My heart is thumping so hard my chest begins to hurt. I can't be responsible for anything bad happening to Charlie. I have to fix this. I lean back in my seat, clutching my chest. *What have I done?*

"What's wrong? Are you having a heart attack or something?" The anger in his voice is still there, buried beneath a layer of genuine concern.

I cough to try to clear the tightening in my chest. I can't breathe.

"I get anxiety attacks... ever since... Frank."

I lean forward to take quick, sharp breaths. But all I can think of is Charlie. I screwed up. I got in way over my head. I should never have agreed to help Knox. Now Charlie's going to pay the price for my stupidity.

"Breathe," Knox murmurs, his hand on my back,

comforting me. "Don't think about anything. Just breathe."

I close my eyes and block out the frantic pounding of my heart. I focus all my attention on each breath. Slowly, I begin to breathe normally and the pain in my chest subsides. I sit up and Knox is right next to me, his thigh pressed against mine, his arm around my shoulder.

He looks worried as he brushes my hair over my ear. "Are you all right?"

I nod even though being this close to him is making my heart race again.

"I'm sorry I yelled at you." He takes my face in his hands and leans his forehead against mine. "I don't want you to get hurt. I just want you to know how serious this is."

The car stops, but I don't bother looking around to see where we are. The driver and the guard exit the car without a word, leaving Knox and I alone. My hands reach up to grab his wrists as he cradles my face.

"I don't know if I can do this," I whisper.

He kisses the tip of my nose. "You can do this, Rebecca. This is justice... for your father."

I shake my head. "I don't believe that. I need to know more about this plan if I can continue. My ignorance puts everyone in jeopardy."

His shoulders rise and fall as he sighs heavily. "You're right. It's time for you to know the truth. But first..."

He plants a soft kiss on my jaw then traces his lips down the length of my neck to my shoulder. "Let me have you one last time. The truth might change the way you feel about me. But you're all I've thought about today."

His hand slides under my skirt. As his finger toys with the lacy edge of my panties, teasing me, the resolve drains from my body. I climb onto his lap and lean in to taste his neck. His hands reach under my skirt and grasp the back of my panties. Without warning, he rips them apart and yanks them out from between my legs.

I reach down to undo his pants. His enormous erection is testing the strength of his zipper. I undo his belt, then his pants and soon he springs free beneath me.

I let out a shrieking gasp as I mount him. "You're so hard."

"That's because you drive me crazy."

He thrusts into me as I rise and fall on top of him. The combination of both movements driving him deeper inside me than I thought possible. Each time he hits my cervix, I cry out in pleasurable pain. The most exquisite pain I've ever experienced.

"You always have," he whispers against my neck.

"What?" I say, clutching his hair so I can bring his mouth to mine.

"You've always driven me crazy," he mutters into my mouth. "Since the day you kissed me in your living room."

I pull my head back to look him in the eye and he's

wearing a barely noticeable grin. "It *is* you."

He nods. "Don't stop," he says, grabbing my hips as he grinds into me. "I've been dreaming about you for ten years. Don't stop now."

I rise slowly then come down even slower. Savoring the delicious friction. The way his thick cock stretches me and fills me like no one else.

"Marco," I whisper in his ear and his cock jumps inside me. "Fuck me, Marco. Make me come."

My pussy is pulsing with my need for him when he roughly throws me onto my back across the seat. He pushes my shirt and bra up and takes my breast into his mouth. His tongue flicks my nipple and his soft moans get me wetter by the second.

"Oh, Marco."

He kisses a hot trail down my belly, pausing when his face is between my legs. I'm aching, pulsing for his mouth. Ready to shove his face into me. When he licks me so softly I'm certain I'm imagining it.

"Please. Make me come," I beg.

"Say my name." He licks me again, leaving me utterly unsatisfied. "Say my fucking name!"

"Marco," I breathe.

"Like you mean it."

"Marco!" I cry. "Please, Marco. Don't stop."

His lips and his tongue are hot on me, drinking my juices, sucking my flesh, devouring my aching clit as if I were a succulent last meal. He tortures me in this fashion. Practically tearing at my flesh one moment, then lovingly licking and soothing me the next.

I can't believe this is happening, I think to myself as my body convulses violently. I can't believe I'm having the most intense orgasm of my life with Marco Leone.

He doesn't give me any time to recover from this orgasm. He climbs on top of me and thrusts into me, so hard I scream. Everything about him is electric. His skin against mine. The look in his eyes. His kiss.

His kiss is the one thing I've never forgotten about him. I've dreamed about it for years. And now I know that I'll do anything not to lose it again. Anything.

16

ONCE WE'RE DRESSED, and we've caught our breath, we enter the garage. I'm pleased to find a long table and four chairs where we can sit this time. My legs are like jelly right now.

"Have a seat," Knox says, motioning to the chairs.

I gladly take a seat in the metal chair nearest me. "So, are you going to tell me everything now?"

He sits down across from me and I can sense something has shifted. The animalistic hunger and the tenderness I saw in the car is gone. His gaze is hard and calculating. A mask of coolness.

"I think I've shared more than enough with you, Rebecca. I think it's time for you to start being honest with me."

"But I already told you everything."

"You didn't tell me everything."

"I told you everything I know about Frank Mainella!"

"You didn't tell me about August Simmons."

My stomach clenches at the mention of his name. "What about August?"

"Don't play coy with me, Rebecca. Tell me what you know about August's family."

"What? I... I really don't know what you're talking about."

Then it dawns on me. Is this what I would have found in the file Charlie gave me, if I had taken the time to read it?

"I swear I don't know what you're talking about," I insist. "Please, you have to believe me. All I've ever known about August is that he comes from money. I've only met his mother twice when she visited Manhattan to have lunch with us. They live in Connecticut. I know nothing about them."

I reach across the table for his hand and he sits back so he's out of my reach. "Why should I believe you?"

"Because I'm telling the truth."

"How do I know you're telling the truth? Prove it."

The door to the corridor clicks and I whip my head around to see August enter. "Yeah, Becky. Prove it

KNOX

volume 2

CASSIA LEO

1

A WARM HAND lands softly on my hip as smooth skin presses against my back. His hand eases forward until it covers my abdomen. I open my legs a bit, beckoning him to slide his hand lower. His lips are on my shoulder, so warm and tender. I wiggle my hips a little. Rubbing myself against him. I want him to know I'm ready.

"Knox." My voice is barely a whisper, strangled by my desire for him. "Please."

"I love hearing you beg."

His words are a hot whoosh of air in the curves of my ear. My skin pulses, my clit aches for his touch. He keeps his hand pressed against my abdomen as he sucks on my neck. I'm trembling like a junkie. My body coursing with adrenaline and hot with anticipation.

"Please."

I try to push his hand down to where I want it, between my legs. He grabs my wrist and presses his hips against mine. His erection is hot and hard against the back of my thigh. I want it hot and hard inside me.

He's going to make me beg.

I slip my hand free of his grip. Then I reach back and grab the back of his neck as I turn my head around to kiss him. His kiss is as powerful as every other aspect of his being. It's possibly the most powerful weapon in his arsenal; though I'd never tell him that. Knox is not the kind of man who wants to be known for his kiss.

"Please put it in," I murmur this plea into his mouth.

He gently massages my breast and a spark of pleasure pulses between my legs. He squeeze my nipple, tugging it lightly. I arch my back, never letting my skin lose contact with his hard cock.

"Please put it in where?" he asks, and I can hear the smile in his voice.

"Please fuck me in my ass."

His hand slides down and I let out a high-pitched cry as his finger teases my clit. Then his erection slides between my thighs, finding my wetness. He rubs his thickness against my flesh until his cock is slick with my juices. He prods the entrance to my ass and I gasp.

He slides in no farther than an inch and groans. "Fuck!"

The burn of my flesh being stretched is consuming. It fills my body with a savory warmth that oozes into my limbs, rendering me useless. He pulls out slowly. I close my eyes and swallow hard in anticipation. He enters again, a bit farther, his finger massaging my clit so my muscles contract around his cock.

"You're unbelievably delicious," he murmurs into my ear. "Absolutely fucking unbelievable."

He goes slowly, moving a little farther with each stroke, until he's buried as deeply inside me as my body will allow. Until I can feel the tip of his hard cock prodding my abdomen from within. My eyes roll back in my head with sheer ecstasy. I can't speak or move. I can't even tremble as the orgasm rocks me. I've died a most exquisite death.

He fills me with his essence as he explodes inside me. The warmth of it oozes over my cheeks and my body is too spent, too limp to care about my sheets. If I could, I'd lay here in this position forever.

It takes a good hour to recover from this episode enough to invite Knox to shower with me. I scrub the solid muscles of his back as he leans with both hands splayed on the wall. I massage his neck and shoulders a little and he moans with pleasure.

"You're so tense." I dig my fingers into his shoulders and they're hard as granite. "You need a massage."

"There's ten years of hatred packed into those

muscles. No masseuse in the world that can fix that."

I slide my arms around his waist and lay my cheek against his back as I think of the day I discovered the extent of his hatred. The day I discovered that Knox will stop at nothing to avenge his mother's murder. The day I found out just how far he'd go to get to me.

When August walked into that garage three weeks ago, I was certain I was hallucinating. I didn't believe August and Knox could be in on anything together. They couldn't be more different if they were born on different planets.

August is a spoiled rich boy who summers in the Hamptons and blogs about vintage fashion. Knox is a polished billionaire with a penchant for domination and a deep connection to the Veneto crime family—*my* family.

When August sat down at the table in the empty garage and told me that he had been working with Knox for five months, my heart nearly stopped. It was all beginning to make sense. August hadn't invited me to his apartment in four months. He was just stringing me along for months until the day before my father's arraignment. Then Knox could initiate the phase of his plan that involved me.

I didn't speak to Knox for more than a week. Didn't answer his calls, emails, or texts. When he showed up at my apartment, I didn't answer the door. I knew he wouldn't knock down the door. He doesn't want to draw attention to himself.

But I'm not stupid. I know that he knows I must be handled gently and often from a distance. I'm the key witness against my father. As long as he keeps me happy, his vendetta can continue without any snags.

The problem is that I know I don't have that much leverage. Even if I testify that I saw my father murder Frank Mainello in my living room when I was thirteen years old, Knox will find a way to have me discredited. Not because he's an asshole. But because nothing will stand in the way of his revenge.

So I watch what I say and do. He watches my every move. I can feel his presence everywhere I turn. Knox knows all my patterns and vices. All my family. All my coworkers and friends.

Friends.

Discovering that August was in on this plan threw all my relationships into question. Wasn't it my best friend Lita who asked me to walk her to the train station where I was abducted by Knox's goons? Wasn't it Lita who made me question August's fidelity with a single question?

Did Knox get to Lita too? That's exactly what I plan on finding out this afternoon.

Knox turns around in the shower to face me. He takes my face in his strong hands and kisses me, as if he knows what I'm thinking about. And he just wants me to forget everything except him and his maddening kiss. It works.

He lightly sucks on my top lip as he pulls away.

"Delicious." He flashes me a cunning half-smile as he slides his hand between my legs and pushes me against the shower wall. "I'm taking you to see your father next week."

Shoving two fingers inside me, his thumb caresses my engorged clit. Shockwaves of pleasure pulse outward all the way to my toes and fingertips. He takes my earlobe between his teeth and growls in my ear.

I laugh as a chill passes through me. "I don't need to see him."

"This is not a request, Rebecca."

He pulls his fingers out from between my legs and slowly lifts it up. He gets my leg all the way up so he can lay a soft kiss on the inside of my ankle as he pushes his cock inside me. He holds my leg up by the ankle as he thrusts into me slowly. The friction of his cock on my clit sends shivers through me.

"I don't want to see… my father in jail… for the rest of his life." *Moan.* "But I also… don't want to see my father."

He pounds into me so hard I feel as if he might rip me in half. "He goes to trial in two months…. You're going to see your father…. I'm taking you myself." Maintaining his grip on my leg, he laces his fingers into my hair. Then he gently yanks my head back as he pounds me even harder. "On my plane."

He tightens his fist around my hair and tugs. My

mouth falls open in a tiny gasp. He shoves his tongue into my mouth, silencing me. Proving I have no choice in this matter. Knox does what he wants. And *I* do what he wants. So next week I'll go with him to see my father, the murderer, for the first time in four years.

2

KNOX'S VOICE BLARES like a siren in my mind, warning me not to tell Lita anything about him or his involvement with August and my father. Of course, Lita has been texting and calling me non-stop for the past three weeks from her parents' house in Poughkeepsie. Since my father's arraignment was broadcast on national television. She would have come back to Manhattan sooner if it weren't for my insistence that I really am okay.

Lita and her purposely frizzy light-brown hair attack me the moment I open the door to my apartment.

"Rebecca! I'm so sorry I left you!"

She shakes me like a child hugging a rag doll. At five feet eleven inches tall to my five-foot-seven stature, this is a very accurate simile. I laugh as I hug her back. Though my laughter sounds a bit strained by her crushing hug—and my suspicions of her.

She finally lets go. "I'm so sorry I wasn't here when it all went down. Especially since August turned out to be a total prick, as I suspected."

She takes a seat at the small metal table with the formica veneer. I take a seat across from her and push a glass of iced tea toward her. Lita doesn't drink often. One of the many things I admire about her. She has an insatiable need to control a situation and alcohol works against that need. I have to figure out how to control this conversation. How to steer it toward the truth about whether or not Knox has involved her in his vendetta, while also steering clear from the truth about my involvement with Knox.

She sniffs the air dramatically. "You had sex in here, very recently."

"What? No, I haven't." I grab the sweaty glass in front of me and take a sip of my iced tea.

She glances over her shoulder at the unmade bed. "You're lying. Who was it? It wasn't August, was it? You're not back with that cheating prick, are you?"

"No! August makes me sick. He was probably cheating on me for months."

"So he admitted to it? Just like that?"

"No, I'm just assuming because…."

I take a long sip from my iced tea, trying to stall. I

don't want to lie to Lita about August and his involvement with Knox. Lita has enough trust issues without me piling more on.

We've all been betrayed by someone at some point in our lives. Someone who made us despise people who lie. For Lita, that person was her mom.

When she was seventeen, the woman she thought was her mother introduced her to her real mother. It turned out the woman who raised Lita was a neighbor of Lita's biological mother. Lita's biological mother was young when she had Lita. She literally left Lita on the neighbor's doorstep with a note and took off.

Now Lita spends three weeks every summer in Poughkeepsie with her biological mother, to make up for lost time. Her relationship with the mother who raised her is still strained. But I understand how difficult it is to recover from such a complete betrayal. When I saw my father murder "Uncle" Frank, I felt as if I was finally seeing the real John Veneto. Not the one who pretended to be my loving father.

Then, of course, there's the possibility that Lita already knows about Knox. Why else would she ask about August on the very day I'm abducted by Knox and this whole scheme between August and Knox blows up in my face? It can't be a coincidence. Can it?

"Lita, I have—"

I stop myself when I have a sudden realization. Knox

probably has my apartment bugged. When I asked him if he has me bugged he claimed that none of the surveillance is conducted in my apartment. He said he didn't want his men watching me get dressed. Or listening to me scream his name in the throes of passion. But I'm not sure I believe that my apartment isn't being watched.

"You have... what?" Lita's round gray eyes don't blink as she waits for me to finish this sentence.

I lean forward to whisper in her ear and she giggles like a schoolgirl. "I'm seeing someone new."

"I knew it!" she shrieks.

"Shh!" I almost clap my hand over her mouth. "Please don't say anything... aloud."

She looks at me like I'm crazy. "You're acting very weird. Are you dating that creepy guy from work? What was his name? Charles? Chuckie?"

"Charlie," I reply quickly to shut her up.

A knot of regret twists inside my stomach as I think of my coworker, Charlie. After he saw me coming out of the Queens Forensics Lab when I was supposed to be at home sick, Knox had to "take care of" him. Whatever that means. Charlie hasn't been to work in three weeks. He has been calling into work every few days just to say that his mother, who lives in Michigan, is still not doing well. As soon as Charlie became a liability to Knox, his mother suddenly became ill.

I have a feeling Charlie is never coming back to the

14th Precinct.

I slide my chair across the tile floor so I'm right next to her. Then I lean in close to whisper in her ear. "I'm being watched."

She turns to face me, probably to make sure I'm not bullshitting her. "By who?"

"My dad."

It's not a lie. Knox works for my dad.

Her eyes widen as she realizes I'm not acting weird at all. "Why? Because of the trial? I don't get it. Do you have evidence against him or something?"

"I can't talk about it. But you can't tell anyone. Okay?"

"Shouldn't you report it if you think you're being stalked? You work for the fucking police department. Jesus Christ, Becky. This is very serious."

I shush her again. "I'm not being stalked. Don't freak out. I have it under control."

"You have it under control!" she whisper-shouts at me. "You really think you can control your dad?"

I look her in the eye and will myself not to break down. *Don't tell her what you saw. Don't tell her about Frank Mainella.*

My shoulders slump as I realize I can't keep this kind of secret from Lita. She's the first friend I made when I moved to Manhattan from Bensonhurst four years ago. I met her in a sociology class at Hunter College.

I showed up to class late once and she offered to let

me copy her notes at the Starbucks down the street. She's still addicted to their chai tea lattes four years later. We met at that Starbucks and chatted for hours. We became instant best friends the moment she told me she had just moved to Manhattan from Poughkeepsie to get away from her family. It was comforting to know I'm not the only one with an unbearable load of family baggage.

"Listen to me. I'm not in danger. Like you said, I work for the fucking police department. I'm used to having eyes on me. I know how to handle myself. Okay?"

She runs her hand through her hair then she reaches into her purse, which hangs from the back of her chair. She pulls out something small wrapped in newspaper. I shake my head as I take it from her hand and begin unwrapping. I crumple up the newspaper and toss it onto the table. Then I stand the slender eight-inch-tall cat figurine down between us.

Lita always brings me back a hand-painted cat figurine from a little Polish pottery shop in Poughkeepsie. She did it the first time three years as a joke. I was so creeped out by it that she did it again last year. This is the third one.

"Thanks."

She glances around the apartment and her lips curl into a smile. "You still didn't tell me who you had sex with this morning?"

I sigh as I lean back in my chair and think of my morning with Knox. "It's nothing." I try to be nonchalant, but I can't hide my grin.

"Oh, no. I recognize that look." She leans forward on her elbows. "Is the sex that good or are you in love?"

"I'm not in love."

"So it's the sex?"

I stare at the table so I don't have to look her in the eye. How do I tell her that it's more than sex? How do I tell her I've been pining for a guy I made out with when I was fifteen? She'll think I'm a crazy person. How do I tell her there's no way to describe Knox's energy? You have to be near him to feel it. To be consumed by it.

"It's more than sex."

"You just broke up with August three weeks ago and you're already in love? Spill!"

I look up and meet her desperate gaze. "Knox Savage. He owns a private security firm. He's—"

"He works for your dad."

"Why do you say that? Do you know him?"

Her eyebrow twitches and she shakes her head. "It doesn't take a genius to figure that out." She sits back in her chair and pauses for a moment, lost in thought. "Is he protecting your dad while he's out on bail?"

I nod and think to myself, *Something like that.*

3

KNOX

"MAKE SURE THE rope is long enough for him to stand with his feet firmly planted on the chair, but not so long his feet touch the ground when he drops. Remember: He's six-foot-four on his tiptoes," I issue my order gently.

Billy's a good kid, but he can be a little dumb sometimes. He needs to be reminded how to do his job—often. I don't mind. The kid may be dumb, but he's brutal. He'll do anything I ask of him.

I sit down at a table in the steakhouse around the corner from the 14th Precinct. I watch as Billy sets up the noose a few feet from the table where Charlie and Rebecca sat a few months ago. My tech guy, Sven, already planted the suicide email on Charlie's laptop. He setup an untraceable automated task to send out the email to

Rebecca about one hour before the time of death.

Poor little lovesick Charlie. He just couldn't get over Rebecca. And now that his mom died of ovarian cancer last week, he had nothing left to live for.

Bruno carries Charlie's limp, chloroformed body in his arms like a baby. The pads underneath the cuffs on his wrists will ensure there's no sign of struggle or captivity. Charlie's been kept in a warehouse near his mother's home in Michigan for the past three weeks. We had to allow time for the injuries from the initial struggle to heal. Now he's brand new and ready to die.

I must admit, a small part of me almost wishes he'd wake up from his chloroform fog and try to fight his fate. It's been a bit pathetic watching the video feed of him going insane in the padded cell we created for him in Michigan. It took about nine days of hunger strike for him to break down and begin cooperating. He gained back the weight and did whatever we wanted. Too bad he never had a chance.

Bruno climbs up onto a step ladder with Charlie's body. He sets Charlie's feet flat on the chair. Then he holds him around the waist from behind like he's about to perform the Heimlich maneuver on him. Billy strings the noose around Charlie's neck and Bruno lets his body lean forward into the noose. Now Charlie's standing up on his own, leaning forward with his weight balanced on the rope around his neck.

Bruno climbs down from the step ladder. Billy takes a step back to admire their work. Finally, Bruno moves the step ladder out of the way so he can kick the chair out from underneath Charlie.

"Wait!" Bruno and Billy look confused by my outburst. "I want to do it."

4

KNOX GOT TO Charlie before he could get to anyone else.
I'm grateful that I'm not going to be implicated in the
mishandling of my father's evidence file. All I did was
misplace the file in the receptionist's desk at the Queens
Forensics Lab. The file was found the next day. Right after
my father had already been arraigned then released on
house arrest and $15 million bail. But I can be charged
with obstruction of justice if anyone finds out I moved
that file.

So I'm grateful that Knox took care of Charlie. But it
still makes me sick to go into work every day and not hear
Charlie's snide remarks. Knox silenced him too. And he
refuses to tell me where Charlie is or if he's okay.

"He's still calling into work, isn't he?" Knox barked at

me the last time I pressed him for information on Charlie.

"That doesn't mean he's not hurt. Where are you holding him? When are you letting him go?"

Eventually, my questioning turned into hysterics. Luckily, we were in my apartment so no one saw my meltdown. Knox has yet to take me out in public. And he still hasn't invited me to his home. He claims it's for my own protection. Like the security detail he has parked outside my apartment building 24/7.

Right now, I just have to concentrate on doing my job. Detectives and officers come in every few minutes to submit new evidence for processing. I log it in and my coworker, Tracy, files it away until someone else comes and picks it up to be transferred to another evidence storage facility. Or a forensics lab for testing. Or a courthouse to be presented as evidence in a trial.

By ten a.m., I'm ready to call it a day. Then everything stops. For more than an hour, not a single person enters the evidence locker. Nobody passes through the corridor on the sub level. Just complete silence.

I'm beginning to notice a pattern.

I pick up the phone to call the sergeant, but the shriek behind me makes me drop the handset. I spin around in my chair and Tracy is covering her mouth, her eyes fixed on her computer screen. The look on her face sends chills through me.

"What's wrong?"

I shoot out of my chair and round Tracy's desk. She quickly tries to minimize her browser window, but it's too late. I saw it. The headline reads: **NYPD DETECTIVE FOUND DEAD IN MIDTOWN RESTAURANT**.

"Open it back up."

Tears are welling up in her eyes. "Honey, you don't want to see that."

"Open it up!"

Her shoulders slump as she reaches for her mouse and clicks the window. It reappears on the screen and with every word I read my body sinks farther down. Until I'm done and I'm crouched next to Tracy, clutching her desk for support.

"Baby, this is not your fault," she insists, but she has no idea how wrong she is.

She thinks Charlie committed suicide because he couldn't have me. She doesn't know the truth. The truth is that Knox didn't just silence Charlie. He killed him.

Charlie was just collateral damage in his revenge plot. How much longer will I last before I too become collateral damage?

I'm not sitting around and waiting to find out

5

THE KNOX SECURITY corporate headquarters on 7th Avenue is pretty much exactly as I imagined it. Tall, dark, and sleek. It exudes strength and security. If Knox were a building, this is what he'd look like.

I storm into the lobby and there are three different receptionists: a blonde behind a glass desk in the center of the lobby; a black girl with beautiful auburn hair behind a counter on the right; and an Asian girl behind another desk on the left. For a moment I'm so confused that I forget how angry I am.

"May I help you?" the blonde girl asks, and all my rage resurfaces.

"I need to see Knox Savage."

She smiles, a knowing smile. As if she knows who I

am or I'm not the first woman to come barging in here demanding to see Knox.

"Mr. Savage is in a meeting. And he only sees people by appointment. Do you have an appointment, or would you like to set one for a later date?"

"I don't need an appointment, so you can wipe that little smirk off your face."

The girl doesn't even have to call anyone or press any buttons and two security guards in suits are at my side.

"Ma'am, what seems to be the problem?" the guy on my right asks in a high-pitched but calm voice.

I hate to name-drop, especially with the way the news has latched onto my father's story, but it seems I have no choice.

"Do you know who I am?"

The guy looks at me. At least, I assume he's looking at me. I can't see his fucking eyes through those dark sunglasses.

"I'm Rebecca Veneto. John Veneto's daughter."

"Shit." He whispers this under his breath, then he turns to the receptionist. "I'll take her up."

The elevator works on a fingerprint and a security pin. When we step inside, the gleaming silver mirrored walls, combined with the frantic pounding of my vengeful heart, make me woozy. I grab the handrail to steady myself.

Charlie is dead.

"Ma'am, are you all right? You look a little pale."

"I'm fine."

When we reach the 29th level, the security guard looks at me expectantly. "I don't have clearance on this level."

"So, what do you mean? You brought me up here for nothing?"

"No, but you do. You just need to place your index finger right there," he says, pointing a small sensor on the elevator control panel. "Then enter your security pin on that touchscreen beneath the sensor."

"But I don't have a security pin."

"We were told that if you came here today to tell you that your security pin is a six-digit number."

I shake my head in disgust. Of course he expected me to come here. He's always one confident stride ahead of me.

I take deep breaths as I attempt to think of what my six-digit pin could possibly be. I place my index finger on the sensor and a numeric keypad materializes on the touchscreen. I try my birthday with no luck. I try Knox's—Marco's—birthday and nothing happens. I try my dad's birthday, my mom's birthday. Nothing works.

Then I remember the last time I saw Marco in my living room when I was fifteen. The day he got out of prison and left Bensonhurst to become Knox Savage.

I enter the date 041806. April 18, 2006.

The elevator doors slide open and I step out in amazement. I can't believe it. I haven't even seen him yet and he's already succeeded in manipulating my emotions. I'm now less angry than I was when I stepped into this building.

Fortunately, knowing that I was manipulated ratchets up my anger once again. I stride across the plush carpet toward the redheaded receptionist with the phony smile.

"Good morning, Miss Veneto. Mr. Savage has asked me to inform you that he is in a meeting, but he will be out very soon. May I offer you some coffee, tea, or champagne while you wait?"

"Stick your champagne and your nasty little smirk up your ass. Where's his office?"

There are two doors on the wall behind her on either side of the desk. Left or right. Which should I choose?

This is not a riddle, Rebecca. Just make a choice.

I head for the door on the right and the receptionist head me off. Her face is almost as red as her hair. She's pissed. Good.

"You can't go in there."

We struggle for a moment as she attempts to prevent me from reaching the door handle. Her skinny fingers are latched onto my right forearm like crab claws.

"If you don't let me go right now, I'll make sure Knox doesn't just fire you. I'll make sure he destroys you."

Even as the words come out of my mouth, I'm horrified. What's come over me?

I'm turning into my father's daughter.

She immediately lets go of my arm. She's terrified.

"I'm so, so sorry. I don't know what came over me."
She reaches for my arm. "Oh, my goodness. Did I hurt
you? Oh, no. I'm so sorry. I didn't mean to do that. I
reacted very badly. Please, please, *please* don't tell Mr.
Savage. *Please.* I need this job."

She doesn't need this job. She needs to get the hell
away from Knox Savage before this job ruins her life. But
I don't tell her that. I pity the girl, but I'm also still sort of
pissed at her.

"Just take me to his office and Knox will never know
what you did."

She nods and opens the door. She holds it open for
me to enter. And now my stomach is acting up again as the
picture on the *New York Times* website flashes in my mind.
It was a picture of the bottom half of Charlie's body
dangling above the place where he and I shared a meal
four months ago. And it finally hits me.

Charlie's dead and it's all because of me. It's all my
fault.

The tears come so fast. My hands tremble as I wipe
them away. We walk down a long, nondescript corridor
lined with dark-gray steel doors. At the end of the
corridor, the receptionist turns to me.

She's stunned by my tears, but she manages to find her
words. "This is his office. He's not really in a meeting."

"I didn't think so."

"Please don't tell him."

"I won't."

"Thank you," she whispers, then she heads back in the direction we came.

I wait until she's out of sight before I reach for the door handle. But the door swings open before I even touch it. Knox is standing just inside the door wearing one of his many tailored Dolce & Gabbana suits. He looks impressed.

"Good morning, Rebecca. That was a sexy little scuffle you got in back there." I try to catch him by surprise with a hard smack to the face, but he grabs my wrist. "Looks like you still have some fight in you. Come in."

He yanks me inside by the wrist then slams the door shut.

"How could you do it?" I shout at him, landing a hard thump on his rock-hard chest with my free hand. "You killed him!"

But he quickly takes that wrist and presses my wrists together. His fingers are my handcuffs.

"Keep your voice down." He issues this warning in a deadly whisper that raises the hairs on my arms. "I did what I had to do to protect you."

"Bullshit! You did what you had to do to protect yourself! And your stupid plan! It's all about your fucking plan!"

"I said keep your voice down!" he roars.

"What are you going to do? Kill me. Am I getting in the way of your revenge? Is it time for me to down a bottle of pills or something? How do I die, Knox? Or Marco? Or whatever the fuck I'm supposed to call you? You're not the Marco Leone I used to know. If your mother knew the things you were doing, she'd be turning over in her grave."

His chest is heaving with animalistic rage. His eyes filled with a fervor to strike out at me. He's spent ten years working on this plan to avenge his mother's death. He won't let me get away with bringing her up.

Or will he?

He lets go of my wrists and my arms flop to my sides. His eyes close as he hangs his head and suddenly I feel guilt creeping into my psyche. How could I bring up his mother?

"I'll never know what my mother thinks of who I've become. And that's why I can't let Tony get away with it. He took everything from me. Her life. Her love. Even her disappointment with my mistakes." He opens his eyes and looks up at me. "I can't let him take you, too. I have to finish this and I have to keep you safe."

The tears come again as I'm flooded with a sickening relief. Charlie's dead and I'm to blame. And I'm relieved.

Knox takes me into his arms as I weep. My tears soak his collar as my body is wracked with sobs of grief and guilt. Finally, I compose myself and pull my face away from the crook of his neck.

"This is very difficult for me to accept," I whisper through my dying sobs. "And this is even more difficult to say. But... thank you. Thank you for protecting me."

He smiles and kisses my forehead. "Now I just have to find a way to protect you from yourself. You caused quite a scene out there. Not that I didn't expect it."

"You always know what to expect, don't you?"

He gazes into my eyes for a moment, pondering this question. "I never expected to find you again."

I wrap my arms around his shoulders and he kisses me slowly. He wraps his arms around my waist and lifts me gently off the floor then carries me to his desk. With one swift swipe of his arm, he clears the entire left side of the desk and sets me down. All the while, his lips never losing contact with mine.

He takes my face in his hands. He infuses a bit more passion and urgency into his kiss and instinctively I wrap my legs around his hips. His hand finds the button of my black skinny jeans I wore to work this morning. He undoes the button and unzips my pants in two seconds then I kick off my heels.

Pulling his mouth away from mine, he quickly lifts me off the desk to stand me up on the floor again. He yanks down my jeans and my panties then tosses them aside. Then he sets me back on his gleaming glass desk. The surface is cool against my bare ass, sending a thrill straight to my pulsing core.

He shoves my knees apart as he kneels before me and plants a soft kiss on my clit.

"Oh, God."

"Lie back, baby." I lie back as his tongue takes another blissful swipe at my aching nub. "And you don't have to keep your voice down anymore. I want to *hear* you come all over me."

6

CHARLIE'S FUNERAL SERVICE is scheduled for next week. The same day that Knox plans to take me to visit my father. I don't know where my father is hiding out. Or, rather, where Knox is hiding my father. But I know that the captain will understand why I don't want to attend the service.

No one has any reason to believe that Charlie's sudden trip to Michigan or his suicide had anything to do with my father's case. They all believe he committed suicide because of me.

By some merciful twist of fate, Charlie's suicide email got caught in my spam filter. I don't know if Knox engineered it that way—to spare me the anguish. What I do know is there is probably nothing Knox doesn't know about me. Which means he was able to log in to my email account and erase the email before I even knew it existed. When he told me about this I was livid.

"It's an invasion of my privacy! How can you not see that?" I shouted at him from the kitchen sink where I was busy washing the dishes from the meal I just cooked for us.

Oh, I saw the resemblance. As if I were channeling my mother's spirit. Standing there bitching at Knox about his shady business practices. As though my childhood wasn't just haunting me; I was reenacting it.

"Would you rather have stumbled across that email yourself? I did it to protect you. If it weren't for me you'd be in a fucking cell or blaming yourself for Charlie's suicide."

"I *do* blame myself!"

It didn't take long for Knox to win this argument. And I wound up nestled against his warm body. My muscles stretched and warm like pulled taffy. Clinging to him. My heart pounding and hair tousled like a desperate child. The after effects of another earth shattering *lesson*.

If someone recorded a video of me in these moments of passion, I doubt I'd recognize myself in the footage. I become someone else when I'm with Knox. I surrender myself to him. Not just my body. I surrender my choice. There is no choice but to do everything and anything he wants in those moments.

I find myself fantasizing about him all day. When will I see Knox again? When will feel his energy lighting up my insides? When will I find my solace in the sweet surrender? Because he knows exactly when to push me harder and when to ease off. When to lay on the punishment and when to soothe my wounds.

Now, as I sit in Central Park watching the world pass me by, the guilt over Charlie's death sits at my side casting a dark shadow over me. All I can think is that I need to be punished. And there's no one who can do it better than Knox.

The walk back to my building is invigorating. I bound up the steps to my apartment buoyed by my excitement. I'll text Knox the usual message: *The birdie got out of her cage again.* I won't even have to cook or order in tonight. We'll dine on each other.

I love having a day off in the middle of the week!

Turning the key in the lock, I immediately notice the lock is loose. It's unlocked.

I take a step back. I've lived with my father long enough and watched enough movies to know that you don't enter your home in cases like these. I glance around the short corridor at the other two doors on this floor.

My heart is jackhammering against my chest. But through the thrumming of my pulse, I can hear movement inside my apartment. The door swings inward suddenly and I nearly jump out of my skin.

7

AUGUST IS WEARING a puzzled expression. As if he wasn't expecting me.

"You asshole. You nearly gave me a heart attack." He chuckles as I shove my way past him. "What the hell are you doing in my apartment? I thought you gave me all the copies you had of my house key."

"Your landlady let me in." He shuts the door and follows me into the kitchen. "I brought you something."

"August, you have to leave. You shouldn't be here."

I grab a glass from the cupboard and fill it up with water from the tap. He watches silently as I guzzle half the glass. I slam the cup down on the counter and glare at him. He's not leaving.

"What did you bring me?"

He smiles and I feel a slight pang of longing in my chest. Apparently, the last four months of my relationship were a sham. I was furious about this initially. But I still find myself missing the lazy Sundays in my apartment. Him complaining about his blog partners while I indulged in hours of bad reality TV.

He grabs a cream-colored box tied with a black ribbon off the breakfast bar. Then he sets the box down on the counter next to me. He looks so pleased with himself.

"Open it," he says as he picks up the new cat figurine Lita gave me and smirks.

"What is it? A severed head?"

"Just open the box."

I untie the ribbon and lift the lid. It's the red scarf I saw in Vogue magazine last month. On one of those lazy Sundays. I didn't even mention it to August. He must have seen me admiring it while I was reading. Typical August to notice me coveting a scarf.

"It's vintage Hermes," he says, pulling the scarf out of the box and laying the cat figurine on top of the cushiony tissue paper. "It will look stunning with that vintage sheath dress you bought a couple of months ago. Very Jackie O."

I shake my head as he drapes the scarf over my neck. "You shouldn't have bought me this. I can't accept gifts from you anymore, August."

"Why? There's nothing wrong with a simple gift between friends."

He's still holding each end of the scarf. The way his eyes keep shifting to my lips is making me nervous.

I remove the scarf from around my neck and push it into his chest. "Take it back."

"Becky, it's just a scarf. It's not a ring."

I march around him and make my way to the dresser near the foot of the bed in my studio apartment. "Just leave."

"Fine. I'll take it back."

He follows after me and I turn on my heel before I reach the dresser. "What do you want? Are you trying to get me back or something? What is this?"

"I want to fucking apologize, okay!"

August has never raised his voice at me. He's always so agreeable. Even when we did disagree, we never really fought. He believes in talking things out calmly. So this outburst is both shocking and exciting.

"You already apologized."

"Not properly." He wiggles his fingers as if he's itching to hit something. "I messed up. I know. But it was only once."

"August, I don't want to know how many times you've cheated on me."

"You're not being fair. Just hear me out."

"I'm not being fair? I'm not being fair? Was it fair for you to fuck someone behind my back?"

"I never *fucked* her!" His green eyes are desperate with

a need for me to hear him out. "Yes, I took her to my apartment, but I never had sex with her. As soon as she left, Knox showed up and threatened me."

"And I'm supposed to believe that you never fucked her because…?"

"Because it's true!" He grabs both my arms and the look in his eyes frightens me. "He threatened to have my uncle killed. He helped my uncle escape the country last year, a few months after we started dating. My Uncle Stewart was about to go to prison for fifteen years for securities fraud. Knox is the only one who knows where my uncle is. We get occasional encrypted video messages from him, but they're all routed through Knox Security so they're untraceable."

He lets go of my arms and grabs my face so I can look him in the eye as he continues. "This is the guy you're sleeping with. He's fucking diabolical, Becky. You don't know what you're getting yourself into."

My stomach twists at the thought of how August and I must look right now; his hands cradling my face at the foot of my bed. If Knox walked in at this moment, he'd probably kill us both.

"You have to leave. Now!"

I push him away and march toward the kitchen. He follows closely behind me. I grab the scarf and the box off the kitchen counter. Then I shove it into his gut.

Opening the front door wide, I sweep my hand

toward the exit. "Thank you for the gift, August, but I can't accept it. Please don't come back unless you're invited."

He narrows his eyes at me as he passes over the threshold. "You've changed. The Becky I knew would never get involved in something like this."

"That's because I'm not the Becky you knew. I never was. I was pretending. I'm Rebecca. Rebecca Veneto. Goodbye, August."

He reaches into the box and hands me the cat figurine. "Tell Lita I said hi."

8

LITA IS SUCH a lightweight. She drinks maybe four times a year. At weddings or on New Year's Eve she'll have one glass of champagne and declare herself "warm."

But guilt is a powerful emotion. I'm going to guilt Lita into having drink number two tonight. I need to know just how much she knows about Knox and August.

Knox's vendetta looks very much like an impressionist painting viewed up close. I need Lita to fill in some of the missing details. Or help me take a step back so I can make some sense of it. If that's possible.

I pick up Lita at her apartment in Chelsea then we head to The Park, a restaurant-slash-dance club featuring indoor trees and shrubs. After yesterday's excursion to Central Park ended in a bad run-in with August, I figured

I'd better cancel out that experience with a trip to a classic hangout.

Lita and I used to go to The Park almost every weekend before I met August. It will be nice to spend some time with my best friend in our old stomping ground. And Knox is busy tonight. Probably off planning something "diabolical." I know his goons are watching me, but we're just here for a drink. I'm not worried.

I pull Lita past the indoor trees that glow with twinkling lights. She protests as I drag her up the stairs, past a display of a dozen or so glowing lanterns. I'm taking her to the second floor bar and dance floor.

"I don't want to dance tonight," she pouts. "I'm hungry! I want some chicken wings."

"We'll get some chicken wings tomorrow. I'll take you out to brunch for a hangover cure."

"Oh, nuh-uh!" She shakes her head adamantly as I pull her through the dense Saturday-night crowd toward the bar. "You have lost your mind if you think you're getting me drunk."

"Please just have one drink with me?" I plead while trying to find a place to squeeze in at the bar.

"I'm going to the restroom. Stay right here. I'll be right back."

Lita wouldn't ditch me, would she?

I turn back to the bar and try to squeeze into a tiny space between a young guy who's wearing some yummy cologne and a blonde who's using her *assets* to try to get the bartender's attention. The guy scoots back a little so I can squeeze in next to him and I smile at him to acknowledge his kindness. He's actually kind of hot. Or maybe it's just really hot in here.

"I've been waiting here for thirty minutes," he shouts a few inches away from my ear. "He's finally getting our drinks. What are you drinking?"

I should decline. I don't want to give this guy the wrong idea. There is no doubt in my mind that I belong to Knox. But how? As a fuck buddy? As a co-conspirator? Or is it something more? Is what we have... love?

We certainly haven't made any verbal commitments to each other. There's no harm in letting someone buy me a drink. Actually, there's no harm in letting this guy buy Lita a drink. Once he sees Lita, he'll be much more interested in her.

"Two Long Island Iced Teas," I reply and he responds with a tiny nod. He's got this.

The bartender returns with three beers—I'm assuming the other two are for his friends—and he spouts off my drink order.

"I'm Alex. What's your name?" he asks, turning around.

He raises his hand to get his buddies' attention. Across a writhing sea of dancers about ten bodies deep, two guys acknowledge his gesture and make their way toward us.

"My name is Lita!"

Alex and I turn toward the sound of Lita's voice. Her lips are pursed and her head is cocked. She does not look pleased.

I hand her the drink. "Look what Alex bought you. Isn't that so nice of him?" I turn to Alex and he's mesmerized with Lita's supermodel looks. "Alex, this is my friend Lita. She's celebrating a promotion today and she needs a little encouragement. She doesn't drink often."

Alex smiles, revealing a mouthful of straight, white teeth. Perfect. Lita insists that guys with gnarly teeth always have bad breath and don't know how to kiss. I nudge Alex's shoulder to break his trance.

"Oh, yeah. Hi, Lita. Very nice to meet you."

He offers Lita his hand to shake and she rolls her eyes. She squeezes in next to me at the bar so that I'm between her and Alex.

"I'm hungry."

"I can get you something to eat," Alex offers, shouting over me as if I don't exist.

His two friends arrive and Lita and I are introduced to Hugo and Barry. Neither or these two are Lita's type, but I would expect her to at least be friendly to Alex. After a few awkward moments of silence and ignored questions, Alex gives up on Lita and asks if I want to dance.

Lita hasn't taken a sip of her drink yet. I don't blame her really. This has got to be the strongest Long Island

Iced Tea I've ever had. And I've had many. I only took two sips of mine before I abandoned it on the sticky bar.

"Sure," I reply, then I turn to Lita. "Just one dance then we can go downstairs and eat, okay? Come on."

"I'll just wait here." She winks at me as Alex and I set off. She knows she's being a pain in the ass, but she's happy she'll be getting her way soon.

The thumping beat of the song rattles my chest. Soon, the music and the smell of sweat and Alex's dance skills have me swaying and writhing along to the beat. I miss dancing. I'm not much of a club person. But dancing brings out a whole other side of me. That primal instinct embedded in my DNA; a part of me that once enjoyed dancing around a fire outside a cave.

Alex puts his hands on my hips and I press my back into his chest. Our bodies move together in time with the rhythm of the music. I slide down, shaking my butt as I go, then I slide back up. The guy dancing next to us smiles at me as he watches us grinding against each other.

Then suddenly I feel something prodding my backside. He has an erection. I spin away from him and that when I see Knox standing at the bar with Lita. Watching me.

Time stops as the club disintegrates. All I can hear is the frantic thrum of my heartbeat. All I can see are those blue eyes glaring at me from across the room.

Alex grabs my arm as I try to leave. "Sorry. You just

got me a little hot."

I shake his hand off me and head for the bar. Knox whispers something in Lita's ear then heads for the stairs. I shove my way through the crowd, my body shaking with adrenaline. Lita looks worried as I approach her.

"What the fuck was that?" I shout at her. "Why did he leave? What did he tell you?"

"He just said to tell you he'd be outside."

I race toward the stairs and through the various rooms until I finally land outside on the sidewalk on 10th Avenue. I glance up and down the street, then I see the black SUV. It's parked in front of the pizzeria on the corner.

The driver steps out as I get closer, to open the door for me. I stare at the open car door nervous about what awaits me inside. I just have to remember to stand my ground. I did nothing wrong.

I take the driver's hand and he helps me step up into the backseat of the SUV. Then he promptly closes the door behind me. Knox's gaze roams over my body from head to toe. As though he's trying to gauge whether I've been tainted by Alex's touch.

"We were just dan—"

"Shh!" He turns toward the driver, who's just pulling away from the curb. "Take us home."

"I don't want to go home! I want to talk about this."

He glares at me, his chest heaving. Then he shakes his head as he turns his attention to the crowds on 10th

Avenue.

"We're not going to your apartment. We're going to mine."

9

THE DRIVE TO Knox's place is eerily quiet. I keep my eyes on him the whole ride there, but he only looks at me occasionally. I can't decide if he looks disappointed or if he's silently calculating his revenge inside that dark mind of his.

Finally, we reach his gorgeous pre-war townhouse with a white stone facade and enormous black front door. I would have expected something a bit darker for Knox. But this definitely suits him. It's almost palatial. Fit for a king.

"Wait here," Knox says, grabbing my wrist before I can reach for the door handle.

His skin on mine takes my breath away. It's been less than two days since I last saw him. Yet it feels like this is the first time he's touched me in weeks.

I nod and he lets go of my wrist as he exits the vehicle. The front door opens as he climbs the steps and he disappears inside. The door closes behind him and we wait, the driver and I, in silence.

When the door opens again, Knox's jacket and tie are gone. He opens the car door for me and extends his hand to help me out. My stomach flutters at this simple gesture. Maybe he's not upset with me or maybe he's just buttering me up to punish me when we get inside. Either way, I'm thrilled with anticipation.

He closes the door behind me and leads me up the steps into his home. It's as extravagant as I imagined it would be. This is a level of opulence he never would have achieved if he'd stayed in Bensonhurst doing small time gigs for my father.

The chandelier hanging from the twenty-foot ceiling is dazzling. The creamy white wallpaper with the barely noticeable taupe pinstripes. The custom woodwork, the curved staircase, and the dark furnishings all strike a perfect balance of glamor and permanence. Glitz and comfort.

"This is gorgeous."

He gazes at the abstract painting above the mantle for a moment, then he turns to me. "Come with me."

I follow him toward the staircase, but he passes right by it. He pushes a bookshelf on the wall beneath the stairs.

A soft click sounds and the shelf hisses as is opens towards us. My mouth goes dry when I see another staircase that descends into total darkness.

He flips a switch on the wall and the wooden staircase is revealed to lead down to a well-lit corridor. "Are you afraid?"

I look up at him and there's a slight twinkle in his eye. The possibility that I might be afraid pleases him.

I shake my head. "No."

He smiles at this reply. "Good. Let's keep going."

We descend the stairs and head down the corridor until we reach the second to last room on the left. He pushes the door open a little and flips a light switch. Then he throws the door open all the way so I can see inside.

"If I had known you enjoy dancing so much, I would have brought you here sooner."

The room is the size of a large bedroom. Plush loveseats line three walls. And in the center of the room are two stripper poles extending from the tile floor to the ceiling. The flashing lights bounce off the walls and the intermittently spaced mirrors.

"You want me to dance for you?" I ask.

He closes the door, leaving us standing in the gray corridor. Then he nods toward a door across the hall from the dance room. "You're going to dance for me. But not yet. First, you need to be taught a lesson about freedom. It seems you didn't learn this lesson the last time I tried to teach you."

He opens the door and my jaw drops. In the center of the room is a glossy black table about two feet wide and six feet long. The table is topped with a white vinyl cushion. It looks almost like a fancy doctor's examination table. But the items on the walls tell me Knox is not about to give me a medical exam.

Various chains, whips, ropes, and leather restraints hang from walls. The light glints off the chains and the buckles on the restraints. My entire body floods with a pulsating fear, making the lights dance in front of my eyes.

"Are you afraid now?"

I turn to him, grabbing his arm for support. That's when I notice his sleeves are rolled up. He's ready to go to work.

"I know you'd never hurt me."

"Define *hurt*." He flashes me that devious half-smile and my knees weaken. "Take off your clothes and lie down, Rebecca."

He unzips the back of my dress in one swift motion and a gust of longing sweeps through me. I try not to let him see how my fingers tremble as I pull off my dress. But I know he can see it. He's feeding off of it.

Once I'm naked, he swoops me up in his arms and gently lies me down on the table. The vinyl is cold against my skin. My nipples instantly perk up. Knox notices this and he brushes his thumb over my right nipple.

"This belongs to me." He squeezes it gently and the pulsing need between my legs intensifies.

He pulls two armrests out of the table. Then he covers my wrists in plush sheepskin before he ties my arms down. I shiver as he traces his finger down my belly, over my thigh, and down to my ankle.

How is he going to tie down my ankles?

This question is answered quickly when he pulls out two metal stirrups from the table. He places my feet in the stirrups and ties down my ankles.

"Are you comfortable?" he asks, his voice isn't as gruff as it normally is. There's a soft, reassuring quality to it. He wants me to know that I'm safe.

"Yes."

"Good. Close your eyes."

I do as I'm told and the darkness is both soothing and exciting. I wait for what feels like an eternity before I finally feel his touch. It feels like the soft tassels of a leather whip being lightly dragged over the skin between my breasts. I want to open my eyes, but I know this won't go over well with Knox.

He drags the tassels over my belly and down between my legs. He lands a swift whack against the inside of my thigh and I cry out.

"Holy shit!"

Immediately he holds his hand over the spot where he whipped me and the warmth of his hand makes the pain melt away. He doesn't give me any time to breath before he whips the inside of my other thigh. He takes the pain away with his hand and I brace myself for the next lashing.

The next two land on my butt, one on each cheek. Each time I cry out just as loudly as the last time.

"Does that hurt?"

"Yes!"

He whips my ass again, but this time he gets a piece of my engorged lips. I shriek just as a soft blow lands on my clit. This knocks the breath out of me. Immediately, his mouth is on my swollen nub, soothing me, licking my wounds.

My shrieks turn to cries of pleasure and my legs begin to tremble. He sucks on my clit and kisses every inch of my flesh. But he stops just short of making me come. This sweet torture lasts for at least an hour. Finally, he ends this torment by giving me three successive orgasms.

He has to carry me to the dance room when he's done with me. My limbs are like limp spaghetti in his arms. He lies me down on one of the sofas, then he kneels next to me.

He cups his hand over my sensitive mound and growls in my ear. "Who does this belong to?"

"You," I breathe, completely spent, but I manage to reach out for him. I wrap my arms around his neck and pull myself up so I can hold him close. "I'm yours. Only yours."

10

WAKING UP IN Knox's plush bed, with his lush body lying next to me, is beyond dreamlike. This must be heaven.

I scoot closer to him and he begins to stir. I drape my right arm and leg over his warm body and he pulls me flush against him.

"Good morning, gorgeous," he murmurs.

He lays a soft kiss on my forehead and I return the gesture with a lingering kiss on his scruffy jaw.

"Good morning."

"I have to go to work soon."

"On Sunday!"

He chuckles and the sound is so warm, I want to wrap myself in it. "I work every day. But I'll be back in a few hours. Make yourself at home. The staff will get you anything you need."

I trace my finger down the middle of his solid chest, then I kiss his nipple. "I love… being in your house."

I pull my head back a little to watch his reaction. He's wearing a soft smile as he looks out the window. I grab his chin and turn his head so he's looking at me.

"But I still feel like we're hiding."

His smile disappears. "Of course we're hiding. There's a lot at stake here. No one can know my true identity. Your father doesn't even know."

"But I just want to do something normal. I want you to take me to dinner or a movie or something. Isn't that what you want? To feel *free* for a little while?"

"Rebecca, I'll never be free until this mission is complete. Once Tony's out of the picture, you and I can go to any restaurant or movie theater in Manhattan. We'll dance naked in fucking Times Square if that's what you want. But right now, it's not possible."

I lie back on my pillow and stare at the ceiling feeling utterly defeated. Knox turns onto his side and lays his hand on my belly.

"Okay, listen. I'm finding out today if everything is set up for you to meet your father on Thursday. If I get the green light, I'll take you on a date tonight. Deal?"

"A date? Like a real human date?"

"A real human date. I'll even bring you some flowers if you want."

I turn onto my side to face him again and he immediately reaches around to rest his hand on my ass. "It's a deal."

He lands a soft swat on my behind, then he slides out of bed. "How are you feeling today? Sore?"

I gather the comforter between my legs to fill the void left by his absence. "I feel great." I slide my hand between my legs to check how sensitive I am after last night's lesson.

He tilts his head at me. "Are you touching yourself?"

"Just checking to make sure everything's okay down there."

I squeal as he pulls the covers off me and tosses them to the floor. "I'll be the judge of that."

11

I DECIDE NOT to hang around Knox's house. I'm not one to lounge around and do nothing unless I'm with someone. So I ask one of his driver's to take me to my apartment, then I change into my workout clothes and head for the gym. I need to make sure I'm in pique physical condition for whatever Knox has planned for tonight—and for many nights to come.

I get lucky and find an empty elliptical machine right when I arrive at 11:30 a.m. I drape my towel over the display so I can't see the number of minutes I've been on the machine. This helps because it allows me to keep going past a set time of thirty or forty-five minutes. I just keep going until I can't take it anymore.

It also helps when someone accuses me of hogging the

machine. I can say, "Whoops! My towel was covering the timer. Sorry."

I'm only on the machine a few minutes before someone calls my name from somewhere behind me.

"Rebecca? Is that you?"

I glance over my shoulder and find Lenny Pastore. Lenny worked for my dad until the shake-up in 2004 when Tony Angelo and a few of his guys went rogue. Lenny was about the same age as Marco when Marco's mom, Ella Leone, was killed by Tony in a bad deal. Tony was trying to get some information from Ella. I never found out what kind of information he was gunning for, but he killed her in May 2004.

The weird part was that he didn't try to get away with it at first. He beat the crap out of her and stayed put until the cops got there to arrest him. He was covered in her blood. There was no denying he did it. But he tried to use my dad's name in his statement to the police, saying that my father ordered the hit.

Lenny Pastore was one of the few guys my father ordered to leave the neighborhood after Tony escaped from the courthouse. Lenny spent a lot of time with Tony before the murder and my father didn't want anyone around if he didn't trust them one-hundred percent.

I stop pedaling and step off the machine. "Hey, Lenny. How are you doing?"

He looks way too excited to see me. His thinning

brown hair is slick with sweat. His brown eyes are wide with anticipation.

"Hey, you look great!" he says. "I heard you were in Manhattan now, but I didn't know you were right here in midtown. Where are you staying?"

"Hell's Kitchen. Where are you staying these days?"

"Oh, you know. Here and there. I just got back from the Bahamas. My wife wanted a summer vacation. You know how it is. You're married, right?"

I grab my towel off the machine and drape it over my neck. "No, I'm not."

"Really? I could have sworn I heard you were with some hotshot guy… Knox… Knox Savage?"

"Where did you hear that?"

"Oh, just around. I heard his company was handling the security detail for your dad's bond."

I squint at him, unsure if I'm hearing him correctly. "I don't know anything about the conditions of my dad's case or his bail. I haven't spoken to him in years. And I don't know anything about Knox Security."

"But I didn't say anything about Knox Security."

Shit.

"Well, I don't know anything about them, but I've heard of Knox Savage. I mean, everyone has, right?"

He cocks an eyebrow as if he's caught me in a lie. "Yeah, right. Well, it was good seeing you. Hope I'll see you around again."

I nod as he walks away, cursing myself for making such a stupid mistake. What if Lenny is still in contact with Tony? What if that whole conversation was just Tony fishing for information on Knox?

I'll have to tell Knox about this conversation during our date tonight. Somehow, I don't think this will elicit the good kind of punishment.

12

"WHERE ARE YOU taking me? I'm beginning to wonder if I should be afraid of that devious smile."

"You have nothing to fear tonight," Knox replies as the car whisks us across Manhattan. "I'm taking you to Coney Island."

"Coney Island? But—should you be anywhere near Brooklyn?"

"Relax. There's a reason you didn't recognize me when you saw me in that garage four weeks ago. I've had some work done."

"Yeah, but your eyes give you away."

"To who? Do you think any of the guys from the neighborhood spent hours dreaming about my eyes the way you have?"

He smirks and I smack his arm. "You think that's funny?"

"No. I think it's beautiful." He leans across the backseat and holds my chin as he lays a soft kiss on my jaw. "But not as beautiful as you."

I press my lips together to hide my stupid grin. By the time we get to Coney Island, I'm on hyper-alert for any of our old friends and neighbors. Most of them are married with kids now. So Sunday night is probably not the most popular night for them to come to Coney Island. But I'm still very nervous.

The instant the car pulls into the parking lot at the Brooklyn Cyclones ballpark, my nerves subside. This was one of my favorite places to go as a kid. My dad would always take me to a couple of games in the summer. Until the shakeup in 2004. But I don't ever remember Marco coming with us.

Knox helps me out of the car and keeps a hold of my hand as we walk toward the park entrance. "You once told me about how your dad used to bring you here. You said it was your favorite place in all of Brooklyn."

"I did?"

He laughs. "Yeah, the time I came to the shop and you were stealing some soda cans out of the cooler. You held the cans against your cheeks. You were all sunburned. I asked you what you were doing and you said you were cooling off."

"I remember. That was the day we met."

"Yeah. I was seventeen and you were twelve. Always off limits."

"Until now."

He chuckles then nods at the guy at the ticket counter. "No, you're still off limits. But I've worked my way around that tonight."

The guy behind the counter nods toward the entrance and we enter without showing any tickets.

"You don't even need tickets here, huh?"

"You'll see why."

He holds tightly to my hand as he leads me past the gates and through the maze of people making their way to the stands. Eventually, we end up on the Brooklyn Rooftop at the top of the stadium overlooking left field. This space is usually packed with summer partiers, hence the nickname "the party deck." But we're the only ones up here.

There's a slight breeze in the air now that it's almost seven p.m. With the smell of the ballpark and the sounds of the crowd below us. Something about this night feels magical.

We walk to the edge of the rooftop and I grab the guardrail to look down at the people below us, jostling each other to get to their seats. "This is the best date I've ever been on."

"It's only just begun, baby."

We spend most of the game standing next to each other. Until the seventh inning, when it starts to get nippy. Knox stands behind me with his arms wrapped around my waist. Occasionally nibbling my ear or brushing his lips over my neck. I feel like a lovesick teenager. And I've never felt better.

The Cyclones win and we leave the stadium in great spirits amongst a crowd of people, half of them cheering rowdily and half of them looking like the walking dead. Dying to get home and get to bed before they start their workweek tomorrow morning. Like me.

"I have to get home," I say as we head out of the stadium.

"Just one more place." He smiles and his eyes twinkle in the moonlight. "I promise it will be quick."

He leads me down the path toward the boardwalk. It's almost ten p.m. Most of the shops on the boardwalk will be closed right now, even though it's summer. They're only open late on Fridays and Saturdays.

I don't mention this. I let him take me on a long walk down the boardwalk from the stadium toward 10th Street. The crowds thin out the farther we get from the stadium. Then they get denser the closer we get to 10th.

We pass Luna Park and 10th Street and he smiles when I sigh. "We're almost there."

Finally, we arrive at the aquarium and I'm not surprised to find that it's closed. He moves up close to the decorative metal cutouts. Reefs, fish, seals, and sea plants all cut out of sheets of metal and painted a beautiful sea green adorn the entrance to the aquarium.

Knox looks behind a coral reef cutout on the left and smiles. "Come here."

I squeeze in next to him and he hoists me up onto the rail that surrounds the park. It's at least a twenty-foot drop to the park floor below, but I know Knox won't let me fall. Right there on the backside of the coral reef are the following words written in black permanent marker: *Wait for me. ML 04-18-06.*

Tears well up in my eyes. Even though he never told me about this, I feel slightly ashamed that I never knew it was here.

"I wrote this here eight years ago after I left your house." He sets me down on the boardwalk then reaches up to brush a tear off my cheek. "I never did see your father that day, but I think it worked out for the best. He might have convinced me to stay."

I smile at this. "Yeah, he could be very convincing."

"Rebecca, the last time I saw you, you promised you'd wait to give yourself to someone who deserved you. I hoped that you'd see this message a long time ago, or that this mission would be done years ago. And I could come back to you before you belonged to someone else." He cradles my face in his hands and plants a gentle kiss on the tip of my nose. "I wanted to be your first. But now I realize that it doesn't matter, as long as I'm your last."

He gazes into my eyes, waiting for me to confirm this. And I can think of no better way to do that than with the kind of kiss we shared eight years ago.

Despite the fact that I have to get up at the crack of dawn to be at work the next day, I can't let Knox go home without showing him how much I appreciate everything he did for me tonight. When we enter my apartment, I almost expect to find August or Lenny waiting for me. I never told Knox about my conversation with Lenny. I'll tell him tomorrow.

13

IT'S A FEW days late, but I decide to take Lita to brunch on Tuesday. I ask for a personal day and head down to the Financial District. Lita works for an investment firm where she makes in her words, "pretty decent money." She doesn't have to take a day off when she wants to take a three-hour lunch.

We meet at the only place I know in this neighborhood with good brunch. It's the same place where I met August and his mother for brunch about seven months ago. The food was fantastic, though the company was a bit stiff.

After sitting at my table for more than ten minutes, I call Lita to see where she is. I get her voicemail, but I don't bother leaving a message. Instead, I send her a text.

I set my phone on the table and pull out my face powder to do a touchup. The sound of August's voice makes my shoulders lock up.

"Rebecca, what are you doing here? I thought you were working today."

Rebecca?

"I have the day off," I say, standing up. "So nice to see you again, Mimi."

August's mother, Mimi, is standing next to him in a baby-blue Chanel pantsuit. His right eye is twitching, almost winking at me. I take that to mean that his mother doesn't know we're broken up yet. And he doesn't want me to tell her.

Mimi reaches her bony arms toward me and bumps her cheekbone against mine. Even her flowing blonde hair smells like Chanel No. 5. She steps back and looks down her nose at me with the usual phony smile.

"This isn't your usual hangout. Is it, Becky?"

I smile and pause for effect. "No, actually I'm meeting a friend."

August's eyes flash with horror. He's expecting me to say that I'm meeting Knox.

"Well, don't be rude, August." Mimi elbows him in the arm. "Offer to pick up their tab or something. Whatever it is you kids with blogs do these days."

I cover my mouth as I chuckle and August rolls his eyes.

"I'm just meeting my friend Lita," I clarify for August's sake. "But she's late. I think I may just head on out. I have errands to run."

"Oh, nonsense. Join us in the garden room," Mimi insists.

"I really can't. But thank you for the offer. You two have a beautiful brunch."

I take one last sip of my iced water and I'm suddenly overcome with a wave of nausea. I lean over to kiss to August on the cheek.

He takes the opportunity to whisper in my ear. "Thank you, Rebecca."

I try not to look as if I'm running out of there, but it's hard when I'm practically running out of there. I explode out the entrance doors onto the sidewalk and release a small spew of bile onto the pavement.

August appears at my side. "Are you okay?"

"What are you doing out here? Go back in there with your mom." I swipe the back of my hand across my mouth then push his hand off the small of my back. "Go, August."

"Are you sure you're okay?"

I look into his green eyes. Then I look at the black SUV across the street. Why do August and I keep running into each other? Well, technically, this is the first time. The last time wasn't really a run-in. Still, I can't help but feel as though August is watching me.

"I have to go."

I take off toward the CVS on Fulton as I silently do the math in my head. I got my period the week after I met Knox. It's been about three weeks since then. Is it possible for me to be pregnant?

Knox said he couldn't impregnate me. Did I really make such a rookie mistake?

14

I ENTER CVS and immediately head for the feminine products aisle. I find the pregnancy tests and, instinctively, I look around me to see if anyone is watching. Sure enough, a man in a dark suit passes by the mouth of the aisle slowly. His sunglasses pointed straight at me.

Did Knox lie to me? Or did I just misunderstand him?

I grab six different tests and power walk to the checkout lane. The clerk pretends not to judge me as she scans my items and asks if I have a discount card I'd like to use.

"No," I reply curtly. *Obviously, I'm in a hurry, lady,* I almost say.

I almost expect Knox to be waiting in a black SUV outside the store. Ready to whisk me away to a location where I can pee on a stick in private. But I can't even see the security car anymore. I walk around the corner toward the subway station and head home.

15

I'VE BEEN STARING at the six boxes lined up on my bathroom counter for more than an hour. I've read the back of each box twice. But I still can't decide which one to open first. Or if I should open any of them.

Knox wouldn't lie to me about something like this. I'm only one day late. That's nothing to worry about.

An hour later, I toss all the tests back into the CVS bag and head for Knox's office.

⌒⌒

NO ONE TRIES to stop me when I insist on seeing Knox today. He's not expecting me this time. And I'm keeping my cool with everyone; even the weird redheaded receptionist on the top level. She allows me to escort myself to the last office down the long, gray corridor.

I knock on the door and the sound of Knox's laughter makes my skin prickle. Is his laughter genuine? Is any part of Knox real?

I wait a little more than a minute before he barks at the door. "Come in."

Good. He doesn't know it's me. I finally get to catch him by surprise.

I enter his office and he smiles as he leans back in his chair. His gaze falls to the plastic bag dangling from my hand and he nods. He *does* know why I'm here. Of course he does. One of his guys saw me buying the damn tests.

"You think this is amusing?" I say, holding up the bag.

"I think you're overreacting. I told you I'm not capable of getting you pregnant."

"What do you mean by *not capable*?"

"I mean that I had a fucking vasectomy last year!"

I swallow another pocket of bile. "You *what*?"

"I was in a dark place. I thought I'd never find a way to get you back in my life. You had your new preppy boyfriend and I had nothing but one-night-stands. Every girl I fucked was just a stepping stone on my way to you, but I felt like those stones were leading me farther away."

He leans forward and rests his head in his hands as he stares at the surface of the glass desk. "I didn't see any point in taking chances. If I accidentally got a girl pregnant while wearing a condom, I knew I'd never love that child the way I'd love our child. Then I'd be just like my fucking father. For all I know, that's why my father left. Because my mom and I were only second-best. And he couldn't stand the sight of us."

I set the bag down on one of the chairs and round the desk. I kneel next to his chair. "Knox, look at me."

"No, I'm not done." He heaves a deep sigh. "When I found out about your father's case, I asked the doctor to reverse the vasectomy. He told me that there was a chance I might still not be able to have children, but I didn't care. I told him to go ahead with the procedure." He finally turns his chair and grabs my face. "He said that my body was making antibodies that were killing off my little swimmers. I'd never be able to have children of my own."

I shake my head. "So, it's possible that you're no longer creating antibodies, right?"

"I don't think so. But maybe you should take one of those tests before you jump to any conclusions."

I glance at the chair on the other side of his desk where I set down the bag of tests. "Can you take me home?"

We enter the apartment at half past noon. The summer sun is shining through my sheer curtains. It's at least ten degrees hotter inside than it was outside. I switch on the window air conditioning unit and grab the bag of tests to head for the bathroom, when my phone rings.

I don't recognize the phone number, but I recognize the area code. Someone's calling me from Poughkeepsie.

"Hello?"

"Lita—I mean—Becky. This is Lita's mom, Carrie Matthews."

This had to be the biological mother I'd never met.

"Hi, Carrie! Have you heard from Lita? She was supposed to meet me for brunch an hour ago."

"Becky… Lita's been abducted!"

KNOX

volume 3

CASSIA LEO

1

I BOUGHT THE rundown bistro in the Meatpacking District two years ago. I closed it down immediately, then I got a letter from "a concerned resident." He was worried that I was devaluing the neighborhood by closing down a local favorite. People who concern themselves with stuff like property values and the historical richness of a rundown restaurant are the kind of people I envy.

They don't worry about whether they'll wake up in the morning with the muzzle of a silencer pressed against their forehead. They don't look at every single person they know and wonder if—or when—that person will betray them. And they sure as fuck don't worry that the person they care about most in this world will be killed today, and they'll have no one to blame but themselves.

There are a million reasons I do the things I do. And those are just a few. Avenging my mother used to be the number one reason. Now it's her.

Rebecca is gone. I'll stop at nothing to get her back. And Lenny and Gino know that.

I snap my fingers at Billy as we enter the restaurant. "Dust off one of those tables and take it to the back. And three chairs. Hurry up!"

Bruno locks the door after Lenny and Gino enters behind me. Lenny looks around the dusty restaurant as if he's entered a fucking haunted house.

"What are we doing here?" Gino asks nervously.

Gino's a young kid from the old neighborhood. His father was close to Tony Angelo. Before his father accidentally fell off the Brooklyn Bridge onto a passing tour boat. I'll admit, that was a rookie mistake on my part. But it happened a long time ago, before I knew how to make people talk.

"We're just here to talk," I say, flashing them a chummy smile. "Come on. Let's go sit in the back where we can have a little more privacy."

Gino and Lenny look at each other. They know they have no choice but to follow me. People don't appreciate having their choices taken away. It triggers their animal instincts. That's why you have to keep them calm. Don't let them feel too threatened.

Billy has cleared a large area of the kitchen by pushing

the stainless steel prep tables into the corner. The table and chairs he robbed from the front of the restaurant are now dust-free and standing coldly in the center of the kitchen.

"Have a seat, boys," I direct them as I reach up to grab a few glasses off a shelf. "You want a glass of water?"

Lenny and Gino look at me like I'm crazy. They want me to get to the point.

"I asked you two if you want a fucking glass of water."

"No," they reply in unison.

I nod as I put back the dusty glass. Taking a seat in the third chair at the table, I lean back and smile at Lenny and Gino.

"Do you boys have any idea what I brought you here to talk about?"

They both shake their heads, but Lenny's hiding something. He won't look at me. I wait a moment for the rage to subside, then I continue.

"We're here to talk about Rebecca Veneto. Do you all remember Rebecca? John's little girl?"

Lenny's eyes dart toward my face for a moment, then he looks down at the table again. "Yeah, I remember Rebecca. I... I ran into her the other day at the gym."

"I know. What did you two talk about?"

"If you already know, then you probably know what we talked about." I look Lenny in the eye for about two seconds before he continues. "All right. We talked about you."

"Listen, Lenny. No need to get nervous and clam up. We're just chatting. Okay?" He doesn't nod so I nod for him. "Now, don't make me ask you again. What did you and Rebecca talk about?"

"Nothing, we just—"

"Don't say *nothing*! That's not the way you have a conversation, Lenny."

The silence that follows is wet with their fear. They both stare at the table, trying not to let that fear show. They're feeling cornered.

I chuckle and Gino's shoulders jump at the sound. "Hey, we're all friends here." I can see Lenny cringing inwardly. "I know you all don't know me, but you know my company is handling John Veneto's security detail. And you know Rebecca was abducted last night, right?"

Gino's eyes flit toward Lenny, but he doesn't speak.

I smile at this. "Do you dress like that every day, Gino?"

He looks confused for a moment, then he looks down at the tattered brown T-shirt covering his round belly. "Uh... yeah. I guess."

"You do realize you look like complete shit, don't you?"

"What the fuck?"

"Have you ever stepped on a fucking treadmill? You know, one of those things you run on that makes you feel like you're going nowhere? Do you know what a fucking treadmill is?"

"Fuck you!"

The gun is out of my holster and the bullet is exploding through the back of his head before either of them know what's happening. Gino's body tips sideways toward Lenny, who's eyes are wider than saucers as he jumps out of his chair.

"What the fuck did you do?" he shrieks in his awful whiny voice.

"Sit down, Lenny."

"You fuckin' killed him! What the fuck is wrong with you?"

I lock eyes with Bruno then nod toward Gino's body, which is slumped across the chair Lenny just vacated. Bruno grabs Gino's fat lump of a body off the chair and lays him on the dingy tile floor.

"I said sit down, Lenny."

Lenny's chest is heaving as he stares at Gino. Then he glances around the kitchen. Looking for an escape. But Bruno and Billy are blocking both exits. He looks at me and I nod at the chair for him to sit.

"I... I can't sit there. It's covered in blood."

"Billy."

Billy leaves his station near the back door to wipe off the chair and Lenny begins eyeballing the exit.

"Don't get any ideas, Lenny," I warn him as Billy's

cleans up the blood. "Now sit."

He shakes his head as he takes a seat again. "I don't know where she is. I swear to God. I don't know nothing."

He's going to start crying. I hate this part.

"Well, I suggest you go home and take some fucking ginkgo for your memory. Because I want you to go home and tell everyone who I am. I'm Knox Savage. And I will kill you and your wife if you don't have some fucking information for me the next time I see you." I stand from the chair and nod at Bruno. "Get him the fuck out of here."

2

THE GUY SITTING across from me in my office is an old friend of John's. I agreed to see him as a favor. John Veneto was the only father figure I knew growing up in Bensonhurst. I don't know if Rebecca knows that her father and my mother had an affair that lasted more than four years. If she does, she hasn't mentioned it to me. And that's not like her.

Rebecca wears her emotions like a winter coat. All wrapped up in a cozy, protective layer of anger and lust. It's her standard operating procedure. I don't mind. She's beautiful when she lashes out at me.

"Ahem."

I blink a few times as I realize Mario's trying to get my attention. "So you said your brother-in-law is looking at how many years?"

Mario looks annoyed that I wasn't paying attention. This fucker doesn't know that I don't give a shit about his brother-in-law or the number of years he's going to be locked away. I've got more important stuff to worry about right now. But I can't break cover.

"Twelve years."

"All right. I need you to break down the timeline of the case." I push a pad of yellow paper across the glass desk. "Write it all down, starting from the date of his first crime to today. I need names of accomplices. Addresses if you have them. I need court dates. Names of lawyers and public defenders. I need everything. Write down as much as you can remember. I'll be right back."

I don't normally leave people alone in my office. It's an invitation for people to try to spy on me. But I need to clear my head. I need some fucking news or I'll be useless to Mario. And I can't stop being good at what I do. That's how mistakes are made.

I step out of the office and head straight for the door to the stairwell. Hiding in a stairwell isn't my usual coping method. Usually, when something's bothering me, I'll hit the gym or the shooting range. But this isn't the kind of unease that can be worked off.

I've never felt more lost in my life. Rebecca has been gone for less than forty-eight hours and it's rendered me almost completely useless. Maybe I wouldn't feel so lost if

I didn't feel so responsible.

It happened right after she got that phone call from Lita's mother in Poughkeepsie. A phone call I'm convinced she was forced to make. Because the first thing Rebecca wanted to do after that call ended was to go straight to the police station.

I tried to convince her not to go.

"You can't go to the police station." I grabbed her arm to stop her from storming out of the apartment. "I can't go in there with you. You'll be totally unprotected. Just wait a while. Wait for the police to contact you."

"I can't wait! My best friend has been kidnapped! Do you not understand? Every second counts." She pauses for a moment as her face contorts with anger. "Did *you* do this?"

"What?"

"Is this part of your fucking vendetta? Did you take her?"

"You're talking crazy now."

I grip her arm tighter as she tries to free herself. I can't let her go to the police station in this state. She's liable to mention my name in a fit of rage.

"I'm talking crazy? You're the one who—"

I twirl her around and clap my hand over her mouth before she can say anything about Charlie. Her lips continue to move against the palm of my hand as she protests. Then I remember why we came to her apartment today: so she could take a pregnancy test.

I slowly remove my hand from her mouth and she attempts to stomp on my foot with her spiked heel. I move my foot away and she grunts in frustration when her heel comes down on the carpet.

Keeping my arms locked tightly around her waist, I lean in to whisper in her ear. "Baby, you have to keep your voice down. You can't shout about stuff like that here."

She let's out a soft whimper and begins to sob. "I never wanted any of this to happen. I just wanted to help my dad."

"I know, sweetheart. I know." I spin her around and brush her tears away as I kiss her forehead. "You have to trust me. I'm going to find your friend."

"But I need to talk to them. See if there's any information I have that can help. We were supposed to meet for brunch today. They need to know that."

I grit my teeth because I know I'm not going to convince her to stay away from the station today. She's in law enforcement. She knows the first twenty-four hours in any abduction case are the most crucial. And she's right that every second and every piece of information counts during that time. I have to let her go.

She was only at the station a few minutes before someone grabbed her in the elevator. They took her down to the sub level garage, stuffed her in the trunk of a police car, and sped off.

I haven't been able to get my hands on the surveillance footage, but that's my next mission. Not that I think the footage will reveal anything I don't already know. This whole abduction scheme has Tony Angelo written all over it.

He knows I'm getting close to tracking him down and he's panicking. He's trying to gain the upper hand. He doesn't know I'll always have the upper hand as long as he doesn't know my true identity. He'll continue to underestimate my commitment to bringing him down. My commitment to Rebecca.

Right now, Tony thinks taking Rebecca will raise John's hackles. He thinks I'm just the schmuck that John hired to keep him safely hidden. He's right about John being riled up. I had to talk him out of launching an all-out assault on Tony's family. But Tony's wrong about me. Rebecca's safety comes before John's. Always.

My phone vibrates in my pocket and I stand from the concrete step in the stairwell. I glance at the screen and see Bruno's number flashing. I don't program anyone's name into my contacts. I have an uncanny ability to remember phone numbers and dates. When I look at a phone number, I see a name and a face.

"Yeah," I answer.

"The cops just left her apartment."

"Thanks."

Time to see if I can take this investigation to the next

level.

3

REBECCA'S APARTMENT LOOKS just the way we left it,
save a few missing items. Despite what Rebecca may have
suspected, I don't have cameras in her apartment. But I do
have listening devices planted in her kitchen and a camera
pointed at her front door. And I do remember seeing a
small army of cat figurines on the kitchen counter two
days ago. They're not here anymore.

Traces of black fingerprint powder coat the counter,
the refrigerator, the telephone. It doesn't matter if they
find my fingerprints. Marco Leone's fingerprint records
have been mysteriously lost. The only fingerprints they'll
find here are Knox Savage's.

I touch my fingertips to my left arm where I had the
tattoo of my mother's name, Ella, covered up. You're

probably wondering why I've gone to such lengths to find my mother's murderer. It's simple. I always finish what I start.

When my mother was killed thirteen years ago, I was fifteen years old. It was a gloomy Sunday night in April. The rain was pouring down from the sky faster than the gutters could swallow it up.

I'd been hanging out at my buddy Jerry Mainella's house most of the day, talking to his dad Frank. He had a project he wanted me to work on. Some off the books drug deals. I didn't realize at the time that it was just a distraction. Frank knew I'd go straight to John after I left there to tell him what Frank was up to.

While Frank was spitting bullshit in my ears, Tony Angelo was at my house trying to beat some information out of my mother. I walked in on Tony beating my mother's dead body over the back with the bottom of a steel lamp.

I ran to the kitchen to get a knife. Not to defend myself. I was going to kill him. But he knocked me over the head with that fucking lamp and the next thing I know I'm waking up as the medics put me on a fucking stretcher.

I always finish what I start. And I never got my chance to kill Tony Angelo.

I also never found out what information he was trying to get out of my mother.

Looking at the fingerprint dust fills me with rage. I

hate the idea of anyone in Rebecca's apartment, touching her things, other than me. For all I know, Tony could really have someone at the department working for him. That bastard could have been in here a few minutes ago.

I walk out of the kitchen toward Rebecca's bed. It's still unmade. I sit on the edge and grab a fistful of sheet. I bring it to my nose and breathe in her scent. Like lilac and her own personal musk.

The smell of it instantly brings back the memory of our date to Coney Island. The feeling of her body against mine as I held her so close. Watching the game on that rooftop with my nose buried in her neck. I don't think I've felt that happy in thirteen years.

When we came back to her apartment afterward, I had to stop myself from fucking her. I knew that wasn't what she wanted after a night like that. And I knew it wasn't what I needed.

I needed to show Rebecca that she was more than just a fuck toy. Though she makes a very delicious toy, indeed. I knew we both needed something different. Something foreign to me.

As we walked into her apartment, I locked the door behind me. Then I used my phone to turn off all the listening devices in the apartment. The first time I'd done that since we installed them a month earlier.

I lead her to the bed and she immediately reaches for my belt buckle. I would normally push her hands away.

I've never allowed a woman to take the lead in the bedroom. There are many places where my rule is law, but first and foremost in the bedroom.

I allow her to unbuckle my belt and her eyes widen. Just the sensation of her fingers on my clothing is getting me hard, but I know I have to be patient.

I reach one hand up and brush her hair behind her ear. She closes her eyes, eyelids fluttering at the sensation of my fingertips whispering over her skin. Her hands freeze on the top button of my slacks. Just one touch is all it takes to render Rebecca useless. It's one of my favorite things about her.

I grab her face and kiss the corner of her mouth. She sighs as her hands fall to her sides. I plant a soft kiss on her mouth and her lips part just enough for me to slide my tongue inside. Her mouth opens wider as her tongue brushes against mine. She whimpers as I hold her head firmly in place and breathe her in. Inhaling every needy little sound and breath she issues.

Her hands find the button of my pants again and she hastily unfastens them. Before I can stop her, she's kneeling before me taking me into her mouth.

Her lips are firm and her tongue is warm and wet as she grips the base of my cock and slides it in.

"Oh, baby." I groan as I gently grab a fistful of her hair.

She's careful to wrap her lips over her teeth as she

bobs torturously slowly. Then she grabs my hips and pushes me back. She looks up at me, a devious smile in her eyes as she lays a soft kiss on the tip of my cock.

She massages the underside of the head with the tip of her tongue and my eyes roll back in my head. It's too fucking good. Then she sucks on just the tip with just her lips as her tongue continues stimulating the frenum.

I'm about to blow when she draws me in again. I hit the back of her throat and I have to stop myself from pushing myself further in to choke her. She bobs her head just a few more times until she's swallowed every last drop.

"I want you to fuck me," she says, removing her clothes as she stands up.

"I'm not going to fuck you."

"Why?"

I slip my hand underneath her hair to grab the back of her neck. Then I press my forehead against hers. I want to tell her that I'm not going to fuck her tonight because... because I love her. But I can't force my mouth to form the words.

"Because I'm going to go slow tonight. Okay?"

She tilts her head up to kiss me. I don't normally kiss a woman after she's blown me. But Rebecca is not just any woman. God help me. I'm in way too fucking deep.

I slide her panties off then I lay her down on the bed. I spread her legs and immediately go to work. Sucking gently on her clit, I use my middle finger to stimulate her g-spot. When her hips begin to buck, I know she's getting close. I continue to lick her clit as I slide my finger into her ass. She shrieks and begs for more as she gushes all over me.

Normally, I'd turn her over and fuck her from behind. But tonight is different. I slide up, giving her no time to recover from her orgasm as I lift her left leg and slide into her.

She wraps her arms around my neck and kisses me hard. The taste of both of us mingles and I can hardly breathe from how hot it's making me. I rest one elbow on the mattress then I wrap the other arm around her tiny waist and lift her gently. Then I push into her, hitting her cervix, swallowing her moans.

I want to say it again. I want to tell her I fucking love her. I always have.

I always will.

But I never got the words out. Not even when she came to me, thinking that she might be pregnant with my child. I never told her.

Now she could be out there. Anywhere. Carrying my baby. She could die with my baby inside her and she'd never know.

I push off the bed and begin looking around. The first drawer I open on her dresser is stuffed full of panties and bras, arranged in no particular order. Peeking out from underneath a pair of pink panties I see a stack of pictures.

Pulling them out, I'm somehow not surprised to see a picture of Rebecca and August smiling on a ski lift. This must be the photos she took down after they broke up. I don't know what to think of the fact that she didn't burn them. Maybe she was going to give them back to August so he could get off on them.

I flip through the stack and it only takes six pictures for me to get down to the naughty pictures. The first one is just a selfie of Rebecca and August lying in bed naked, with only a small portion of her breast showing. The next one is Rebecca standing in front of the bathroom door naked. She's looking over her shoulder at the camera as he takes a picture of her backside. The next picture makes me toss the whole fucking stack at the wall.

I slam the dresser drawer shut and grip the edge to try to steady myself.

The pictures were taken a long time ago. I can't allow myself to get worked up like this. I knew Rebecca and August were together. I knew they were having sex. I encouraged it. Until I got a taste of her.

Now she's mine. And I think August needs to be reminded of that after the little stunt he pulled showing up at the same brunch restaurant as Rebecca two days ago.

I dial August's number and he picks up on the first ring, as usual. "I've got a job for you."

4

I ALWAYS ARRIVE early to dinner meetings. If your dinner companion arrives to find you seated at the table, the first advantage of the evening goes to you. They're already nervous because they don't know how long they've kept you waiting. And I'm not the kind of man people like to keep dangling.

When August arrives at Il Conte, one of the four restaurants I own in Manhattan, he looks annoyed. He's not nervous about arriving four minutes late. He's bothered that he had to come here at all.

"Have a seat."

He's wearing one of his ironic faded hipster T-shirts today. Smokey the Bear: Only *you* can prevent forest fires. He wants me to think he's just some small-time blogger who can't be trusted with anything too important.

"So what's this about?"

I chuckle. "Relax, August. Have a fucking drink." I nod at Bruno, who's standing next to Billy behind August's chair. "Tell Mia to get us one scotch and one pint of that new IPA."

"I don't want a drink. I want to know why I'm here."

"You'll like the new IPA. You can write about it on your blog."

Now he's beginning to look uncomfortable. People don't like having their choices taken away.

I smile at this thought and pause for a moment, giving him a chance to speak up. If he's really nervous, he'll say something. If he's only moderately anxious, he'll keep quiet.

He's not nervous enough yet.

"I've got a job for you."

"I'm done. You said you'd get my uncle back into Connecticut. I'm not doing anything until you deliver on your promise."

I glance toward Billy and he nods. August looks over his shoulder at Billy then back at me.

"What? Are you going to have me killed if I don't do what you're asking?"

There are only a few patrons in the restaurant at ten p.m. on a Thursday night. And they're not seated anywhere near us. But I can't let this little cocksucker off so easily.

"I'm only going to ask you once to keep your voice down. If I have to ask you again, you're going to be choking on your marble-sized balls. Got it?"

His mouth is set in a hard line as he shakes his head. "I should have just gone to the police five months ago."

"Good. That's exactly what I want you to do."

He looks at me like I'm crazy. Bruno arrives and takes up his position next to Billy. He's closely followed by a blonde waitress, Shelly, who's carrying the drinks Mia just made for us. I don't employ waiters or bartenders. I only employ women in the front of the house of all my restaurants. It's good for business.

Shelly sets the beer down in front of August. Then she sets my usual tumbler of scotch down in front of me. She flashes me a nervous smile then quickly sets off toward the bar. August's eyes follow her ass for a moment before he turns back to his beer. He's probably contemplating not drinking it just to spite me. But he soon relents.

He takes a long swig then sets the glass down. "What do you want me to do?"

I reach inside my blazer and his eyes widen. I pull out a stack of photos and set them face down on the table.

"First, I want you to go home and cry while you jerk off to those pictures." He stares at the pictures for a moment, but he doesn't reach for them. "Then, I want you to go into the police station and get a copy of that surveillance footage."

"I can't. And you know that."

"Yes, you can, August. And you will. Because that's the only way your uncle's coming back to this country.

5

august

The box-like building known as the 14th Precinct is about as welcoming as an Eastern European orphanage. And under the circumstances, it's about the last place I want to be right now. I have no idea if the police suspect I had something to do with Becky's disappearance. The ex is always one of the prime suspects.

But I know I have to do this. Not just to get my uncle back into the country. I have to do it so Knox can find Becky.

She may be Rebecca to Knox. But to me she's still my Becky.

I enter the police station and find a group of four officers behind the counter, laughing it up while sipping their muddy cups of coffee. I stand at the counter for a moment, resisting the urge to clear my throat, and soon one of the officers looks in my direction.

"Hey, August!" Joe calls out to me.

The faces of the other officers get very serious at the sound of my name. They all turn to look at me at the same time. I don't think I'm imagining the tension in the air and the skeptical looks on their faces.

"Hey, Joe. I'm just here to see Tracy. Is she in?"

I already know she's here. I just spoke to her three minutes ago.

Joe picks his fat ass up off the edge of the desk and saunters toward me. "Yeah, I think she's downstairs. Sorry about Becky, man."

I lower my gaze to the counter as a strange sensation of grief overcomes me. Not a single person has expressed any regret or condolences to me about Becky's disappearance until now. And somehow, it hits me like fucking train.

I grit my teeth against the emotion then look up at him. "Thanks. I'm just here to see Tracy. My mother and I didn't want to leave anything to chance, so we hired a private investigator to assist with the investigation. Tracy said she'd talk to me today. See if she could be of some assistance. Of course, if that's all right. I don't want to overstep."

Joe looks genuinely regretful as he nods. "Yeah, man. You know where she is."

I let out a small sigh of relief as he buzzes me in. "Thanks, Joe."

"Anytime."

I enter the elevator and Joe sticks his arm in to slide his card key in the slot, then he hits the sub level button. It lights up he wishes me luck as the elevator doors close.

I glance around the gleaming steel walls of the elevator. It dawns on me that this is the last place that Becky probably felt safe before she was taken. My stomach twists at the thought of what's happened to her in the last three days.

If she's found alive and I find out she was hurt while in captivity, I'll find a way to kill Knox Savage.

I exit the elevator and Tracy sees me coming before I even reach the door. She shoots out of her chair and greets me at the entrance to the evidence locker. She sobs as she throws her arms around me and squeezes me so hard I can feel my organs shifting inside me.

"Oh, August. Honey, I can't believe this happened. I should have been at my desk. I would have seen it."

"Tracy, this is not your fault." I pry her arms loose and hold her arms. "But you have a chance to help now. Do you have it?"

She nods as she turns and walks around Becky's old desk. She reaches into the top drawer and retrieves a stuffed toy Snoopy in a plastic evidence bag. She sniffs loudly as she hands it to me.

I gave Becky this Snoopy doll when we first started dating after I found out she loves *It's the Great Pumpkin, Charlie Brown*. She used to keep the doll on her desk. Tracy said she stuffed it away in a drawer a few weeks ago. I told Tracy I needed it for the private investigator. Since I can't get into Becky's apartment, this was the only personal item with a lot of her scent I had access to. It was a good lie.

"Thank you."

"My pleasure, baby. Anything I can do to help."

"Actually, there is something else." I pause for a moment and she raises her eyebrows in anticipation. "Do you think I can see the surveillance footage? I want to see if I recognize those bastards."

Her mouth drops open a little as she contemplates this.

"Please, Tracy. It's driving me crazy not knowing where she is."

She covers her mouth as if she's going to start crying again, then she nods her head. "Real quick. Come on over here."

She takes me behind her desk. Then she sits down and types up a bunch of commands to get to the surveillance footage. I hold the back of her chair and try not to make her uncomfortable as I lean over her. I need to get the camera in my shirt pocket at just the right angle to record her screen.

She plays the footage and I hold as still as I can while

she looks away from the screen. She can't bear to watch it again.

The guy smiles at Becky as she enters the elevator, but she doesn't seem to acknowledge him. Then the doors close and he grabs her from behind, covering her mouth with a piece of cloth that's probably soaked in chloroform.

She goes limp in his arms and that's when I finally start trying to memorize his facial features. But it's too late. He's moving too fast as he moves out of the elevator and into the corridor. The surveillance feed switches to the camera in the corridor, but we only get a glimpse of the side of his face before the feed switches again.

This time we see the front of his face, but it's no one I recognize. He's got a fleshy nose and, even in the grainy footage, I can tell his skin is covered in pockmarks. One thing I can say is that his police uniform looks like it was tailored just for him.

Then he disappears and the feed switches to footage from a camera in the parking garage. The police car is already waiting. He stuffs her into the trunk and hops into the passenger seat. Then they drive away in no particular hurry.

I stand up straight and realize I've been biting my lip through that whole video. Licking my lip, I taste blood.

I can't sit back and run errands for Knox. I have to hire a private investigator. I have to find Becky.

I thank Tracy for her help then I thank Joe again as I

head out of the station. As I come out of the entrance, I see a taxi pull up to the curb. I slip inside and Knox and I sit in the backseat in silence until the cab is a few blocks away from the station.

I hold out the pen, but I pull it back as he reaches for it. "This is the last thing I do for you." He doesn't blink as he looks me in the eye. "And you're going to fulfill your promise."

He smiles as I hold the pen out to him again, but he doesn't reach for it. He knows there's more coming.

"And you're going to find Becky. Because you're not the only one with more money and influence than the police force. And you're not the only one who loves her."

His smile disappears as he takes the pen out of my hand and slowly tucks it into the inner pocket of his blazer. He shakes his head and the smile returns.

"You really should not have said that."

6

REBECCA

I OPEN MY eyes and instantly I know something is wrong. I can't move.

My hands and feet are bound with ropes to the iron bedposts. I try to scream, but it comes out muffled and desperate through the cloth tied around my head, which covers my mouth. This is really happening. I've been kidnapped.

I have to assess my surroundings. I have to remember all the details. Someone will find me. Knox will find me and I'll have to tell him everything.

My eyes dart around the space, taking in every detail. A clean white sheet covers the mattress where I lay. The room is dingy and gray, with a narrow beam of sunlight shining through a hole in the foil that covers the window.

Almost as if my captors are worried I'll die without sunlight.

Worried. What a stupid thought. Of course they're not worried. Whoever tied me to this bed is not worried about my well-being.

I try to pull my hands and feet loose from my restraints, but all I succeed in doing is making a racket as the feet of the bed scrape against the wood floor. I stop as soon as I realize how loud I'm being. But it's too late.

The footsteps become louder as they get closer. My heart pounds so hard I can't hear the footsteps anymore. Finally, the door swings inward and my heart drops.

Knox stands in the doorway. I can't see his face, but I'd recognize his silhouette anywhere. He's the one who did this to me.

"Why?" I try to shout through the gag, but my cries are unintelligible.

He steps into the room and closes the door behind him. He's wearing the usual suit attire, minus the blazer. His sleeves are rolled up, but he's not wearing the usual sly grin.

"You have to keep your voice down, gorgeous."

I shout obscenities at him through the gag and he shakes his head as he approaches the bed. "Now, now, Rebecca. I can't remove the gag if you're going to scream. Nod if you promise to be quiet."

I shake my head and fight against my restraints like a

wild animal. He bows his head, looking utterly disappointed with my disobedience. He waits until I've tired myself out. Once I'm lying still, my chest heaving and heart pumping, he finally looks up. I turn away to make him upset and he grabs my face to force me to look at him.

"I'm doing this to protect you and your father, Rebecca."

I try to shake my head to free my face from his grasp, but his fingers only dig harder into my jaw. Then the tears come.

Please. My plea comes as a soft moan through the gag. *Please let me go.*

He lets go of my jaw and brushes the tears from my temples. "Don't cry, sweetheart. I'm not trying to hurt you. I'm trying to keep you safe."

The tears come faster. I don't know if I'm imagining it, but I see genuine regret in his eyes.

"I love you, Rebecca."

My stomach clenches and I close my eyes hoping that this is all a bad dream. Please let this be a nightmare.

"I just want to keep you safe."

His hand is on my belly and I can't open my eyes. I don't want to know what his face looks like when he's lying to me.

His hand slips deftly under my shirt until he has my breast cupped in his hand.

Please stop.

"I love you, Rebecca. I always have."

I realize quite suddenly that I'm only wearing a skirt. No panties. His hand is between my legs.

Oh, God.

He parts my flesh with his fingers, then his tongue is on me. Circling my clit in a slow, tortuous fashion. He finds the most sensitive spot; an area no bigger than a pinky nail. And he stimulates me until I orgasm twice. Until I feel as if I might asphyxiate with desire.

My muscles twitch and ache as he rises from the bed. I open my eyes and he swipes his thumb across the corner of his mouth. The devious smile is back.

"I'll keep your body and your lust well-fed until it's time to let you go. Don't worry, sweetheart."

Suddenly, I'm desperate for him not to leave.

Wait! He tilts his head at my muffled cries. *Wait! Please.*

"Do you promise to be quiet, princess?"

I nod hastily and he sits down on the bed again so he can untie my gag. I let out a soft grunt as the gag is removed and I can breathe freely again.

"Thank you," I whisper breathlessly.

"I'll leave it off as long as you're quiet."

"Please don't go," I plead.

He smiles as he tosses the gag over his shoulder. "You want more."

"Yes."

Suddenly, the restraints are gone and I'm facedown on the mattress. The weight of his body on top of mine is comforting as he moves in and out of me.

"Don't stop."

He hugs my waist tightly from behind as he pushes himself farther inside me. We both grunt in unison as he reaches places he's never been.

"Oh, Knox."

He moves slowly as he aims to dig farther into me with each stroke. Every thrust elicits a louder moan from me as he bites down on my shoulder to keep from coming too fast. Finally, he bites down so hard, I cry out in pain. I look at my shoulder and the blood streaming down to my breast is alarming.

"Knox, stop."

But he doesn't stop. He continues thrusting deeper and deeper. Biting harder and harder.

"Stop!"

"Rebecca, wake up!"

I open my eyes and Lita's face appears above me. My heart is pounding and my throat is aching.

"Was I screaming?"

"Yes. You need to be quiet!" she whispers urgently.

I blink a few times to focus my eyes as I sit up. I recognize the room immediately. It's the basement where Lita and I have been held for the past three days and nights. There are no restraints holding up to the bed. No gags tied around our mouths. But the walls and windows are covered in soundproofing foam.

I cover my face and begin to cry. "When are they going to find us?"

"Rebecca, there's no guarantee they're going to find us."

I don't want to think of the alternative. Lita may like to stay pragmatic about this, but I don't want to imagine that I'll die here in this basement. Though everything I've seen in this place has proven that no one will ever find us unless the assholes who brought me here want us to be found. We're being used as leverage.

I guess I can count my lucky stars that they haven't decided to take advantage of us yet.

Then I think of the dream I just had. I reach up to touch my shoulder and I flinch when Lita puts her arm around me.

"You were having a sex dream about Knox." I chuckle through my tears and she laughs. "It's okay. If anyone's going to get us out of here, it's him."

"How do you know that?"

"Because he loves you."

My mind flashes to the dream again. Knox has never told me he loves me. But the Knox in my dream loved me. He loved me enough to kidnap me and tear open my shoulder as he fucked me. God, I have a sick mind.

"I'm not so sure about that. What if he's the reason

we're here?"

"Come on, Rebecca. Don't be naive. Of course he's the reason we're here."

"Then how can you even claim that he loves me?"

She lets go of me and hugs her knees instead. "Because he's not a monster."

"What?"

"Everything he does is for you."

"No, everything he does is for his crazy vendetta."

"No, you're wrong." She turns her head to look at me through the dim yellow light cast by the bulb that dangles from the ceiling of the dank basement. "He's been paying my stepdad's hospital bills for seven months. And he hasn't done it for his vendetta. He did it so he could get close to you."

"Seven months? And you're just now telling me this?"

"He made me promise I wouldn't tell you. What would you do if your dad was dying and someone offered to get him the best care in the country? What was I supposed to do? Let my dad die? Say *no* to Knox Savage?"

I let out a long sigh as I hug my knees. "It's impossible to say no to him."

"Are you mad at me?"

I shake my head and rest my cheek on my knee. "I'm not mad. I'm scared."

"So am I."

"We have to find a way out of here."

"There is no way out of here. You know that. We've already tried."

"No. We have to strategize. We have to find a way for them to move us. They can't keep us down here forever."

I glance into the corner of the basement where the dingy sink and toilet stand open with no walls or curtains for privacy. Next to the toilet is a stack of about two hundred toilet paper rolls. Just a few feet away is a wooden worktable where we've been eating standing up. A plastic plate of breadcrumbs and two empty plastic bowls sit on the table. Underneath the table there are about forty gallons of drinking water.

We've been surviving on various soups, pastas, and bread rolls. At least the food isn't terrible; even if we do have to eat it with our hands. They must be getting the food from a restaurant. Or they could be giving us a portion of whatever they cook for themselves.

Whatever the case, they don't plan on letting us starve to death. It doesn't even seem they want anything to do with us. Other than sliding our food through the slot in the door, they never interact with us. They don't beat us or threaten us. They don't talk to us. We've never seen their faces. We've never heard their voices.

For all I know, it *could* be Knox out there.

7

BENSONHURST HASN'T CHANGED much in eight years. A good portion of 18th Avenue is closed off tonight for the Santa Rosalia Feast. A food fair Jerry Mainella and I used to love attending, if only because it was a great place to get into trouble and pick up girls.

Some days I still miss this place. Today is not one of those days.

We pass by the shop where John could usually be found sipping sparkling *limonata* and insisting that everyone "sit and eat a fucking meal." Now, he's hiding like a fucking rat in a basement in Newfoundland. We were only able to arrange the terms of his house arrest because his life was in danger. And his lawyer made an excellent case for why I could protect him better than any witness protection program.

We turn the corner and pass up my old house. The house where my mother was beaten to death. A "for sale" signpost stands leaning to the left, as if it's been standing there so long it's exhausted. The grass is a parched beige from the scorching August heat. At least, back when my mother was still alive, people would water the grass if a house was empty. But I guess this one has been empty too long for anyone to care.

It's hard to sell a property where a murder has occurred.

Bruno pulls the car up next to the curb of a white two-story house on 19th Avenue, just down the street from my old house on 80th Street. It's one of the biggest houses in the neighborhood. John bought up the lot on either side of his house so he could expand. The result is an eight-bedroom house with a yard about six times the size of the tiny yard my mother and I had.

Everyone envied the Veneto's house when we were kids. Now I have at least five houses bigger and nicer than this scattered across the globe. But I don't rub my wealth in anyone's face. Especially not John's.

No matter what I've achieved, I'm still the dumb kid that couldn't kill Tony Angelo before he got to me. The one who went crying to John after his mother was murdered. And John will always be the man who killed Frank Mainella for helping Tony escape. All because of a promise he made to me to make Tony pay.

John is a man of his word. It's time for me to become a man of mine.

Bruno opens the gate that surrounds the property and we walk up the pathway toward the front door. He stands to the side, facing the street, as I ring the doorbell. A moment later, I hear light footsteps tapping on the tile just inside the door.

The door swings open and Marie Veneto looks up at me without a smile or a greeting. She opens the door a bit wider and steps aside for me to come in. I didn't expect her to jump for joy when she saw me, but this cold reception only confirms my trepidation about coming here.

"Marie, I'm so sorry about Rebecca."

She doesn't speak as she leads me back toward the kitchen. I follow behind her and the aroma of strawberries and sugar are thick in the air. The kitchen is white and pristine. On the island, a line of strawberry tarts topped with whipped cream is being assembled. I take a seat at the breakfast table as Marie heads for the refrigerator.

She's a tiny woman. Wispy and beautiful, but a powerful presence. She spends all day cooking and baking stuff for people in the neighborhood, but she hardly ever eats any of the stuff she makes. And I can see by the dark circles under her eyes that this situation with Rebecca probably has affected her sleeping patterns as well.

She pours me a glass of lemonade, none for herself, then joins me at the table. Setting the glass down in front of me, she takes a seat and lets out a long sigh. Is she ever going to say anything?

"Listen, Marie. I know I'm not the face you were hoping to see today."

"She hasn't called me in a month."

"What?"

She looks up from the table and meets my gaze. "Rebecca. She hasn't called me in a month. What is going on? Does this have to do with her father? Is this John's fault?"

"This isn't John's fault. This is my fault."

"*Your* fault?"

Her brown eyes widen as she waits for my explanation, and in that moment I see what Rebecca will look like twenty-five years from now. I can't drag this out. I have to tell her the truth.

"Marie, I'm not who you think I am. I'm not Knox Savage."

She shakes her head. "What do you mean?"

"I mean that… I'm Marco Leone."

She squints her eyes as her gaze roams over my face, examining all my features. Her nostrils flare slightly as her eyes begin to water.

"Marco? Ella's boy?"

My stomach drops at the sound of my mother's name.

I nod slowly. "It's me."

She covers her mouth and shakes her head again. "I thought you were dead," she cries. "After Frank died, I kept wondering and asking about you. You were always coming around and then you just disappeared. I thought you were dead." I reach out to pat her shoulder and she grabs my hand. "I want you to know," she begins, the tears falling faster, "that I didn't find out about the affair until years after your mother died and I *never* blamed her. *Never.*"

"I know."

"No, you have to believe me. I've been *sick* about what happened to your mother. I always felt like maybe it wouldn't have happened if I'd been smarter. Maybe if I had found out while it was going on, I could have stopped it."

I don't know why she's making a huge deal about the affair. Everyone in the neighborhood knew that John was unfaithful to Marie. She's making it seem as if she didn't know anything about it. Was she really that clueless?

"Listen. I'm not here to talk about my mother. I'm here to talk about Rebecca."

She loosens her grip on my hand and lowers her head. "The last conversation we had a month ago, I kept pressuring her. I told her she needed to tell her boyfriend to set a wedding date. She kept telling me, "Ma, you need to stop talking about this or I'm never going to introduce you to him.' Then I never heard from her again."

The last thing I wanted to happen during this visit to Marie is get in a fucking conversation about Rebecca and August's wedding. Especially since that little fucker just shot to the top of my hit list. But I have to be respectful. I can't scare Marie. I need her on my side.

"Marie, I'm here to tell you that I'm going to get Rebecca back. And I don't mean back in Manhattan where she'll never call you again. I mean back here, in this house, where you can hug her and measure her for her wedding dress."

"Is she engaged?"

"Not yet."

"Oh, Marco. Bless you." She rises from the chair and wraps her arms around me. "God bless you, Marco. I know your mother is watching over you. I can feel a good presence all around us. I know you're going to bring Rebecca back. I know it."

"I will. If it's the last thing I do."

8

THE LAST THING I need right now is a fucking watery-eyed FBI agent and his chubby sidekick busting my balls over John's case. But cooperating with federal investigations is part of my life as Knox Savage. A life I hope to leave behind very soon.

"Can I offer you two something to drink? Some water, a pop, some bourbon?"

Agent Armstrong blinks his watery eyes as he chuckles. "No, thank you. This won't take long."

I look at his sidekick, Agent Verduta, and she shakes her head, not at all impressed.

Armstrong takes the lead. "So we just have a few questions we need to ask you about John and Rebecca Veneto, then we'll get out of your hair."

Armstrong is playing the role of the good cop today.

"Anything you want to know that's not covered by my confidentiality agreement is all yours."

Armstrong raises his eyebrows. "Confidentiality agreement? Is this something all your clients sign?"

"Yes. It's for their own protection." *From me.*

"Oh, okay. I get it. They have to keep quiet so they don't compromise your security operations, which are meant to keep them safe while they await trial?"

"Look at you, Armstrong. You are one smart cookie."

Armstrong shrugs, pretending to be humbled by my compliment. "What can I say. I've been doing this for twenty-two years."

"Good for you."

Verduta still hasn't smiled or spoken a word and it's starting to creep me the fuck out.

"Okay, I'll try to keep my questions brief and hopefully we won't steer into any breeches of contract," Armstrong continues. "When did you take on John Veneto's case? A precise date, please."

I lean back in my chair and shrug. "I don't know. Sometime in March or April."

Armstrong looks at the notepad in his lap and smiles. "But the charges weren't brought against him until July."

"The investigation and reopening of Frank Mainella's case began in March. And John was always considered the prime suspect."

"Okay. Next question: Was Rebecca Veneto assisting you with John's case at the time of her abduction?"

I take a few beats to maintain my composure. "What do you mean by assisting? Rebecca had taken an interest in her father's case, but I wouldn't say that she was assisting with his security detail."

"Okay. Let me rephrase that. Are you, or *were* you, in a relationship with Rebecca Veneto at the time she was abducted?"

This is where I have to consider getting a lawyer. I don't want to incriminate myself. And the biggest rookie mistake is thinking that you can't get pinched if you didn't do anything. There are plenty of innocent people in prison who will tell you one thing: Never talk to the authorities without a lawyer.

But there's nothing wrong with living a little dangerously.

"Yes. Rebecca and I are together."

Verduta finally breaks into a tiny smile. Armstrong glances at her and they exchange a minuscule nod. Then he writes something on his notepad.

They want me to get nervous and offer more information and justifications, but I'm not a fucking idiot.

"Is that all?" I ask as Armstrong closes the flap of his notepad.

"That's it for now," he says, leaning back in his chair. "Do you mind if I ask you something off the record?"

Off the record. Does this guy think I got this empire by falling for weak ploys like that?

"I don't mind," I say, standing up from my chair. "As long as you don't mind if I grab myself a drink."

"Of course not."

I move to the shelf behind my desk and pour myself a scotch in a highball glass. "So what is it you want to ask me?"

Armstrong glances around my office for a moment, then he looks me in the eye. "Who is Knox Savage?"

I smile at this question, then take a slow sip of scotch. "I'm just a guy with a soft spot for helping people."

He nods and smiles as he realizes he's not going to get shit out of me. He looks at Verduta and nods toward the door. They both stand from their chairs and I offer Armstrong my hand. His handshake is as weak as his method of questioning. Verduta doesn't shake my hand and I'm glad for that.

"You two have a nice day. It's gonna be a hot one." I wink at Verduta as she exits my office. She rolls her eyes as I close the door behind her. "Fucking feebs."

9

QUESTIONS I KNOW I can't answer. Promises I'm not certain I can keep. Accomplices I'm not sure I can trust. Just a typical day in the life of Knox Savage.

Who is Knox Savage?

I lean back in the chair at Mr. Black's Gentlemans' Club and contemplate this question as the first girl takes the stage. This blonde with the loose hips would say that Knox Savage is a hotshot billionaire with a cock the size of her forearm, and he tips well. Bruno and Billy would say that Knox Savage is the one guy in the world you don't want to piss off. Agent Armstrong would probably say that Knox Savage is an alias, though he hasn't figured out anything beyond that.

What would Rebecca say about Knox Savage?

She'd probably say that I've fucked her in more ways than one.

But I haven't fucked Rebecca in five days. I don't usually go this long without a fuck. It messes with my head. But I've never been in a monogamous relationship.

The blonde looks at me and licks her lips as she circles the brass pole. She runs her hands down the sides of her breasts and all the way down to the sides of her hips. Then she turns around and bends over to give me a good view of her g-string.

I can't help but think of Rebecca and the night she danced for me in my club room. We'd just had a breakthrough in the dungeon. She understood that she would never dance for or with anyone but me. So I knew that when she stood up from that sofa in the club room, I was going to get a show.

Her legs were still shaky from the multiple orgasms I gave her in the dungeon as she walks toward the pole. She grabs the pole with both hands and pauses for a moment. Then she turns around and just the sight of her plump breasts bouncing makes my cock twitch.

"Dance for me, baby."

She reaches over her head and grabs the pole behind her, then she slowly sinks down into a low crouch. Keeping one hand gripped on the pole, the other hand caresses her body as it moves down over her breasts, over the soft part of her abdomen, and finally between her legs.

Her eyelids close as her mouth falls open, releasing a soft whimper.

"Knox," she breathes as she rubs her clit, her hips moving slowly backward and forward. "Oh, Knox."

"Louder, baby."

She screams my name as her legs begin to quiver. She screams it over and over again until I feel as if my dick might burst out of my pants. Then she falls to her knees, panting as she crawls toward me.

"That's it, baby. Crawl for me."

Her eyes are on fire with hunger as she grabs my knees and pulls herself up. She straddles my lap and reaches for my belt. I push her hands away and she looks stricken.

"Please," she begs.

"Please, what?"

"Please give it to me. Please let me dance on it."

I smile as I undo my belt and my pants, releasing my erection. She smiles as she pushes off my lap and grabs the head of my cock. She holds the tip against her clit. Then she moves her hips back and forth, using it to get herself off.

"Do you like that?" she whispers.

"Sweetheart, I'd have to be dead not to like that."

She moves her hips forward just a bit more so my cock touches her opening, but she doesn't come down. She's just teasing me. Maybe this is payback for the torture she endured in the dungeon. I'll play along for a little while.

Finally, she lets go of my cock as she comes down and I glide into her. She bucks her hips up and down, back and forth, slowly until she knows I'm about to blow. Then she stops.

She climbs off my lap and turns around. She bends over slowly, giving me a clear view of her swollen pussy. I reach forward and easily find her clit. She moans as I caress her. Then I reach forward with both hands and grab her hips. I pull her backward so I can put my mouth on her.

She's so wet and juicy, and sensitive. She comes in no time. Then I stand up and she knows the drill. She grabs onto her ankles as I push into her. Instantly, my cock is slick with her moisture. I pull out and rub the tip against her clit again. As soon as she begins to moan, I ease myself into her ass.

I thrust slowly at first, stretching her. Then I let her have it. She screams my name more times than I can count before we finally make it upstairs to my bedroom.

The blonde crawls across the stage toward me. "You want a lap dance?" she asks in a husky voice.

I shake my head and that's when I glimpse Lenny on the other side of the club. Getting a lap dance from a brunette in a Dallas Cowgirl outfit.

For shame, Lenny. You're punting for the wrong team.

As soon as I stand up, he sees me and he pushes the cowgirl off his lap. She shouts obscenities at him as he races for the exit. I despise chasing people.

I run after him, pushing a bald guy in a Yankees jacket out of the way. Climbing over a table and hopping over a brass rail. I burst through the entrance and Billy already has Lenny in a headlock in the middle of the parking lot.

I catch up to Lenny and land a thunderous left hook to his jaw. He's out for a minute and Billy and Bruno carry him toward my car. They prop him up in the middle of the backseat of the SUV and sit down on either side of him. I slip into the passenger seat, wrapping my tie around my fist as Lenny's eyes flutter open.

"What the fuck?" he mutters as he reaches for his jaw.

He winces when he feels the swelling. Then he tastes the blood in his mouth and he spits out a tooth into his hand.

"You fuckin' busted my jaw. And my tooth!"

"You shouldn't have made me chase you. I hate chasing people, Lenny."

He spits more blood out into his cupped hand.

"Watch the leather or I'll fucking kill you, you pig."

"Fuck you!" he slurs.

Billy takes him into a headlock again and Lenny's sneakers push against the floor of the car, trying to get some leverage to headbutt him.

"Lenny, you better calm the fuck down or I'll make

you watch as I fuck your wife's brains out."

"All right, all right, all right!"

I nod at Billy as Lenny stops struggling. Billy releases him, but Lenny has to be a fucking asshole and land an elbow to Billy's ribs. Billy clocks him on the side of the head and Bruno and I laugh.

"Take that, you cocksucking piece of shit," Billy says, spittle flying.

I hold my hand up to stop him from inflicting any more damage. I need Lenny conscious.

"That's enough. Now give him your fucking shirt so he doesn't bleed everywhere."

Billy pulls off his jacket and dress shirt. Then he pulls off his undershirt and shoves it into Lenny's lap before he gets dressed again.

Lenny takes the shirt and wipes the blood from his mouth and chin. "What the fuck do you want?"

"You know what I want, Lenny. I want to know who's hiding Tony. If you give me a name today, I'll let you go and I won't fuck your wife in front of you and your kids. I may even let you live to see your fortieth birthday. So what do you say, Lenny? You ready to tell me who's shit-hole I need to look inside to find Tony's weasel ass?"

He shakes his head, but I can tell he's trying not to cry. He already cried in front of me once, and he got away with his life that time. But he's got too much pride to do it again.

"Fuck," he whispers, closing his eyes; resigning himself to his fate. "Nico... Nico Trapani. He's.... He's Geneva's boyfriend."

"I know fucking Nico Trapani."

Geneva Angelo, Tony Angelo's daughter, got herself involved with Nico Trapani a couple of years ago. I should have known there was more to it than her having bad taste in men.

"I don't know where Tony is, but Nico does." He spits into the T-shirt again and he's still bleeding pretty bad. "Can I go now? I swear that's all I know about Tony."

"We'll let you go, Lenny. But first you must be taught a lesson. Because you should have given me this information three days ago."

His eyes widen with panic. "But you wanted to know about Rebecca. I don't know nothin' about Rebecca."

"Are you sure you don't know anything about Rebecca?" I nod at Billy and he twists Lenny's arm behind his back.

"Ow! Motherfucker!"

"Answer the question, Lenny!"

Lenny's cries make me sick to my stomach. I can't stand to see a guy I grew up with reduced to a sniveling rat. But that's all he is now. And even if I don't kill him, someone else will.

"Please. I don't know nothin' about Rebecca. I swear

on my fucking kids' lives. I don't know nothin'!"

I nod at Billy and he lets him go, though I'm pretty sure I heard one of Lenny's bones snap. He'll remember this meeting for a while. And he'll stay quiet about it for as long as he can. At least a few days.

That's all I need now that I have Nico's name. In less than forty-eight hours, Rebecca will be home. With me.

And Tony will be dead.

10

JOHN ISN'T HAPPY that I left Lenny alive. I can take some heat from John if it means that Lenny sweats it out a while longer. Besides, I like the idea of Lenny being taken out by one of his own. It's more poetic.

"All right. I'll see you tomorrow night, John."

"Nothing matters except Rebecca. Don't forget that."

"I won't."

"Good boy. See you tomorrow."

I end the call and tuck the phone into my coat pocket. I'm not actually going to see John tomorrow night. I'm flying to Newfoundland to pick him up tonight. But I can never be too careful. Sometimes even the master must be kept in the dark.

I peel off my jacket and leave it on the backseat. Then

I roll up my sleeves and step out of the car.

As I walk through the corridor toward the garage where I brought Rebecca five weeks ago, I'm struck by the irony or how it all started. And tonight, this is the beginning of the end.

I also chose this location because I knew it would remind me of her. And like John said, I have to remember that nothing else matters. Not his escape. Not my vendetta. Nothing. Except Rebecca.

I enter the garage and the first thing that hits me is the smell. It smells like stale motor oil, blood, and piss. Then I glimpse Nico Trapani sitting on a metal chair in the center of the garage. His hands tied behind the back of the chair and each of his ankles bound to the front chair legs. His head is slumped over and a thin rope of drool is dangling from his mouth.

It's showtime.

"What the fuck is this?" I shout at Bruno.

"You told us to rough him up."

"I told you to rough him up, not to turn him into a fucking vegetable. Are you idiots? Get the fuck out of here!" Bruno and Billy look confused, but they have to. They're good actors. "Get out!"

"Sorry, boss," Bruno mutters as he passes me.

"You'll be real fucking sorry later on. Get the fuck out of here."

They leave the garage and, as the door clicks shut

behind them, I imagine them out in the corridor laughing silently. They're good kids, those two.

I grab another metal chair from the corner of the garage and set it down a few feet in front of Nico, with the back of the chair facing him. Then I straddle the seat and rest my arms on the back of the chair and watch him for a moment.

His light-brown hair is slick with sweat and probably blood. His Knicks jacket is torn at the collar and his gray sweat pants have grass stains on the knees. He must have put up a fight when they picked him up.

"When I was four months old, I fell off the sofa and hit my ear on the wood floor," I begin my story. It's the same story I've used at least a half-dozen times before, but it's very effective. If it ain't broke…. "My mother took me to the hospital and the doctor told her I would probably never hear out of my left ear again. He also told her I would probably have trouble learning how to speak and I'd be behind in all my classes. Basically, he told her I'd be in the fucking cripple classes for the rest of my life."

Nico's chest rises and falls slowly, but he doesn't acknowledge me.

"But my ma wasn't having that. She started me on speech therapy when I was one year old. And she didn't listen when the therapists told her I needed a hearing aid. When I was four, she took me to a doctor who did experimental surgery on me and I regained most of the hearing in my left ear." I laugh as I think of what a crock of shit this story is. "My ma was a real ball-buster. She was a fighter. She wouldn't give up. And by the time I was seven years old, I didn't need any more speech therapy."

I push my chair closer to Nico and he finally looks up. His left eye is swollen shut. His nose is broken and bloody. His bottom lip is split wide open and that's why he's drooling like a baby.

I continue undaunted by his appearance. "So you see, I loved my mother. She liked to help people. So, naturally, I like to help people. And I want to help you, Nick. Do you mind if I call you Nick?" I pause for a moment, but he doesn't say anything. "Of course you don't mind. Anyway, I want to help you get out of this building alive. I want to help your mother, your sister, your girlfriend, and the baby she's carrying, live to see another day. You understand what I'm saying? I want to help you, Nick. But I can't help you if you don't cooperate."

His head falls forward again and I let out a loud sigh as I stand from my chair and kick it aside. This gets his attention and he looks up at me again.

"Fuck you," he mumbles, his words tripping over his fat lips. "And your mother."

I nod as I chuckle. "That's right, Nick. Make this more difficult. That's exactly what your family wants." I turn around and yell at the door, "Bruno! Bring her in!"

Nico's good eye widens as he watches the door. The

metal door swings open and Bruno walks in with Geneva Angelo. She blindfolded and her hands are tied behind her back, but otherwise, she's untouched.

"Genie!" I call out excitedly. "Long time no see."

"What the fuck is this?" she asks as she walks in.

"Let her go!" Nico shouts. "This ain't got nothing to do with her."

"Nicky, is that you? What's going on?"

"Don't panic, Genie. Stress is not good for the baby."

"Who are you?" she shrieks as she attempts unsuccessfully to break free of Bruno's grip.

I walk up to her so she can hear my voice clearly, but I leave her blindfold on. I pull a hunting blade out of my back pocket and Nico watches as I unfold the knife.

"Should I tell her who I am, Nick? Or should I show her?"

He shakes his head and fights against his restraints. "Please don't do this. I'll...."

"What will you do, Nick? Will you tell me what I want to hear or will you tell me the truth? Because I've gotta be real honest with you. Genie won't appreciate it if you lie to me. Will you, Genie?"

I press the tip of the knife to her jaw and she flinches.

"What the fuck was that? Nicky, what's going on?"

"I can't!" Nico roars.

"Listen to your girlfriend, Nick." I trace the knife down her neck and stop when it's just above her belly.

"Jesus Christ," she breathes. "Just tell him!"

If Genie knew what she was trying to convince Nico to tell me, she'd probably rather I kill her and her unborn child. But she won't find out until it's too late.

I smile at Nico as I make a little sawing motion in front of Genie's belly. He gags then vomits a little onto his lap. I've never hurt a woman in my line of work, and I never will. But Nico doesn't know that.

"Fine. But get her out of here."

"Thatta boy, Nick. I knew you'd make the right choice." I nod at Bruno and he hauls Genie out of the garage. Then I retrieve the chair I kicked aside and take a seat in front of Nico again. "All right, Nick. Let's do this fast so we can both get out of here. Where is Tony Angelo?"

Nico tells me the story of his cousin's family who owns a goat farm in Vermont. They've been paid well to keep Tony hidden for the last year as he prepared to return to New York with a new identity. He's running out of cash. And he's tired of living in a basement like a rat.

Nico insists that his cousin's family will be out of the house tomorrow night since they're coming to Bensonhurst for the Santa Rosalia Feast. He swears he doesn't know where Rebecca is, but he knows Tony's definitely the one calling the shots with her.

Nico doesn't know this, but he just signed his own death warrant. I had already planned to kill him, but I thought I'd give him a day or two locked up in this garage to give up some more secrets. Now, I can't risk anything getting back to Tony.

"Thank you, Nick. You've helped me out tremendously."

"Can I go now?"

I stand from the chair and pull it back into the corner. I give myself a mental pat on the back. It's always a victory when I make someone talk without any further bloodshed.

"I told you everything I know. You gotta let me go!"

I exit the garage and Bruno is waiting with Genie just outside the door. "Take her to the loft on Madison. Make sure she's comfortable. She's gonna be there a few days."

Billy looks at me with that gleam in his eyes. He's ready for his instructions. I nod at him then I set off down the corridor as he heads back into the garage. I don't stick around to hear the gunshot.

11

THE FLIGHT FROM Newark to St. John's Airport in Newfoundland is exactly eight hours. My jet gets us there in two-forty-five. As soon as we land in Terra Nova, a helicopter is already waiting to take us to John's hideaway.

John's hideaway. Sounds like a fucking dive bar. But it's not. John Veneto, King of Bensonhurst, has been living in the basement of a farmhouse in the Newfoundland countryside.

I've got a variety of hideaways stashed across the globe. I fly all my clients to and from those locations on my private fleet. We doctor flight logs and sometimes we'll zig-zag the globe in a dizzying pattern to get the high-profile clients from one location to another.

But I'm going straight to John's hideaway today

because he won't be going back there after tonight. Once Tony is dead, John can go home to Bensonhurst and I resume control of the neighborhood. And I can find Rebecca.

And propose to her.

The one-hour helicopter ride over the green countryside is humbling. I don't even know what Rebecca's plans are for the future. Does she want to live in Manhattan forever? Would she like living in the country? Does she want to have kids?

This is all stuff I would have asked her if I'd known she was going to be taken. She would have thought I was crazy, but I don't give a fuck. I want to spend the rest of my life with her. But I want to do this the right way. I'm going to ask John for her hand.

The helicopter touches down just before eleven in the morning. The couple who live on the dairy farm come out to greet me. Mildred and Joshua Raine cover their heads as the helicopter blades slowly stop rotating. Mildred smiles as I approach, not at all perturbed by my sudden appearance.

"Mr. Savage, you look hungry," she shouts over the whoosh of the helicopter rotors.

Joshua holds out his hand and I shake it firmly. "Good morning, Mr. Raine." I turn to Mildred and take her hand in both of mine. "No time to eat today, Mrs. Raine. I've got to get John back home."

"Of course," she replies. "Come inside."

The inside of Mildred and Joshua's humble farmhouse kitchen is uncomfortably warm, as usual. Mildred is always cooking or she keeps a small space heater on in the kitchen to keep it warm enough to rise dough. She bakes her own bread using the grain from an experimental wheat crop planted two years ago. At some point today, she'll complain about the short growing season or the wild caribou crushing her wheat stalks.

"I just took a loaf of sourdough out of the oven. Take it with you, dear," she says, grabbing a round loaf of bread covered in a light checkered cloth off the table.

She tries to hand it to me and I chuckle. "No, thank you, Mrs. Raine. I'm here to pick up John, and that's all. If I eat all that bread, I'll go soft in the middle."

"You need to live a little, Mr. Savage. Life's not all about business you know."

She says this with a wink as she leads me toward the shiny oak door under the stairs that leads down to the basement. Mildred Raine spent a good portion of her life savings to visit me in my Manhattan office three years ago. Her son was on the run. The Canadian authorities and the DEA wanted him on suspicion of drug trafficking. He could feel the net closing in on him and he was staring down forty years to life in an American prison if he was extradited.

I don't know or care if Mildred's son was guilty. All I

know and care about is that, by helping Mildred's son get to a safe house in Brazil, I gained two very important allies in the Raines. And they've been paid handsomely to harbor John for the past five months. The checks they'll receive in the coming years to ensure their silence will more than make up for a bad wheat harvest.

I step into the stairwell and John is already standing at the bottom of the stairs, waiting for me.

"Boy, it's good to see you." He pulls me into a bone-crushing hug and slaps me hard on the back. "I've been going stir crazy down here."

I pull away and take a step back to look at him. His skin is sallow from the lack of sunlight and his belly looks a bit soft from all the bread Mildred's been feeding him. I don't say it aloud, but I'm worried that he's not ready to take on Tony and his goons tonight.

"It's good to see you too, John. You ready to go?"

"As ready as a Bronx whore."

I thank Mildred and Joshua for their assistance and Mildred sheds a few tears when she hugs John goodbye.

"Who's going to eat my homemade pizza now?" she laments as she latches onto Joshua for support.

"Throw a little grass on there and the caribou will eat it," John shouts as the helicopter starts up.

She waves off this suggestion and John and I wave goodbye as we hop into the chopper. The helicopter is too noisy for us to talk. But as soon as the jet takes off from

St. John's Airport, I begin mentally preparing myself to talk to John.

"You look nervous," John remarks as the flight attendant hands him his lemonade. "I don't think I've ever seen you look nervous."

"I've been thinking. Maybe you should let me do this on my own. I don't want to know how it would affect Rebecca if you got hurt."

"Rebecca hasn't spoken to me in four years. She wouldn't know if I got hurt unless she read it in a fucking newspaper."

"Yeah, that's exactly it. She hasn't spoken to you in four years and she still wants to help you. That's gotta tell you something."

I don't want to press too hard, but I really don't think it's a good idea for John to be tagging along on dangerous missions like the one we have planned for tonight.

"Look, Marco. The bottom line is that she's my little girl. And I'm not going to let a lowlife criminal like Tony Angelo use my little girl in his scheme to take over the neighborhood. I'm gonna take that motherfucker down myself. Understand?"

I nod as I take the glass of water from the flight attendant. No alcohol today. I have to keep a clear head until Rebecca is back in my bed where she belongs.

"John, I want to ask you something."

He continues to stare out the oval window. "Shoot."

I lean forward in my seat and take a deep breath. "You know I care about Rebecca a lot."

He turns away from the window to face me. "Yeah?"

I set my glass of water down on the tray and turn my body so my shoulders are facing him. "I'm in love with her, John. I'm going to get her back, not just for you, but because... I want to spend the rest of my life with her."

He narrows his eyes at me as if he's confused. "You want to spend the rest of your life with my daughter? The rest of *what* life? Your life as Knox Savage or your life as Marco Leone?"

"I don't care, as long as it's with her. I'll let her choose."

"You can't let Rebecca choose. She doesn't know what's best for her."

"She's a lot smarter than you think."

I clench my jaw to stop myself from saying something stupid. Like maybe he doesn't know his daughter as well as he thinks he does, since she grew into a woman without any help from him.

"I know Rebecca's smart, but she's never been good at forgiveness."

"She got that from you."

He laughs then takes a sip of lemonade. "I don't know if I can give you my blessing. Your life is not the kind of life I want for Rebecca. I want what any father wants for his daughter. I want her to get married, give me a few grandkids, and live happily ever after. But most of all, I want her to be safe."

"I can keep her safe. You know that."

He looks me in the eye, sizing me up. "Prove it. Get her back. Keep her safe for at least a couple of years. Then I'll give you my blessing."

I smile as my insides fill with warmth. "I will."

12

THE JET TOUCHES down at Burlington International Airport at six p.m. Bruno, Billy, and two of my tactical specialists are already waiting in the chopper on the tarmac. Just as the sun goes down at eight p.m., the helicopter drops all six of us in a small airfield just outside Brownsville, Vermont where three cars await us. Bruno and Billy will take the lead. John and I will be the in the next car with me driving. Jacob and Albert will be in the car behind us, watching for tails.

"You all know the objective. No one strays from the objective," I say once everyone has their weapons packed and their cars ready. "Anyone is fair game, but Tony is mine. If I should go down, Tony is not to be harmed until Rebecca and Lita are found. Understood?"

"Yes, sir," all four of my guys reply in unison.

"Good. Let's head out."

I hop into the black 370Z and shift into gear to follow Bruno's car out of the airfield. The car rides like a beauty on the highway. I may have to get one of these for myself. I don't drive myself around a whole lot because I like to keep my hands free for more important things. But I've always had a thing for cars. My house in Santa Barbara has a ten-car garage and every slot is filled.

I'll admit that leaving all this behind will be hard. But if Rebecca wants me to go back to being Marco, that's what I'll do. I'll do whatever it takes.

"Marco, I got a favor to ask of you."

I glance at John and he's staring straight ahead. "Anything you need."

"If I don't make it out of there today, I need you to promise me you'll take care of Rebecca and Marie."

"Of course I will."

"I know I haven't been the best husband in the world to Marie. She deserves better than me. But I need to know that she'll be taken care of. And I know Rebecca's got a hard head and she's liable to forget about her mother if you don't stay on her."

"I won't let that happen."

"Good. Thank you."

I speed up a bit when I see I'm lagging too far behind Bruno. "Is that it?"

"No, actually, there's something I need to tell you. Something I've been meaning to tell you for a long time." His voice sounds a bit strained. "You've been like a son to me. From the moment I met your mother when you were just eight years old, I knew I'd found the son I never had. You were just like me."

I don't know how to respond to this. I'm not good with emotional stuff.

"When you were twelve, your mom and I broke up for a year. She wanted me to adopt you so you could take my name. I told her I couldn't do that. I couldn't leave Marie and Rebecca." From the corner of my eye I can see him turn to face me. "I know I'm not the kind of father Rebecca wanted and I wasn't the kind of father you deserved, but you'll always be like a son to me. And if anything happens to me today, I want you to know that. Understand me?"

"Yeah, I understand," I answer without looking at him.

"No, you don't understand. Look at me, Marco. 'Cause I need you to understand this."

I turn to face him and there are tears in the corners of his eyes. "And there's something else I need to tell you… about your mother's death. It wasn't—"

His eyes widen at something in the road ahead of me. I don't have time to turn my head before the car slams into something as solid as John's regret.

13

I WAKE UP surrounded by the smell of gasoline. My body's moving, but it's not me moving it. I look up and the bottom of Bruno's square jaw is the first thing I see.

"Let me go!" I shout at him.

"This car's gonna fucking blow!" he shouts back.

And the smell of gasoline hits me again. Shit! I push Bruno off me and scramble out of the broken 370Z onto the grassy terrain. About forty yards south of us is an orange fireball giving off plumes of thick black smoke.

I crouch down to look at the passenger seat and my heart stops. "Where's John?"

Bruno grabs my arm. "He's gone! Come on. We gotta get the fuck away from this thing!"

I push Bruno off me again and glance back at the car

one last time before I walk away.

"What do you mean, he's gone? He was right fucking there!"

The explosion blows both of us forward and we land face down in another part of the field that smells like animal piss. I push up into a sitting position as something trickles down my neck. I swipe my hand across the back of my neck and head. There's just enough moonlight out here for me to see the red glint of blood smeared across my fingers.

"What the fuck happened?"

"A fucking deer."

"A deer?"

"A fucking deer," Bruno repeats. "I slammed on the brakes and you must have swerved to avoid me and landed in this ditch. Jake and Al didn't make it."

"Where's Billy?"

"He went to look for John. The house is less than a quarter-mile from here. We think that's where he went."

"Alone?"

Bruno shrugs and I feel like punching him in the side of his enormous blockhead. He had to slam on his fucking brakes. Jake and Al are dead and John is missing. This plan couldn't be a bigger clusterfuck if I executed it with a group of first-graders.

"We have to go after them. They're outnumbered and out-armed."

Bruno and I load up on ammo and weapons then head down the ravine toward the open pasture. I ignore the woozy feeling I get every time I bend my neck forward. Once I'm done with this mission, and Rebecca's safe, I'll have time to worry about that.

The darkness of night doesn't provide enough cover once we get closer to the farm. From our hiding place behind a large oak tree on the eastern side of the property, I can see that the entrance to the farm is fortified with a well-lit guard station. I can't actually see the guard inside the station from here. For all I know, John may have taken him out. Or the other way around.

We could hop the wooden perimeter fence, but the goats are bedded down near a large building just thirty yards to the south. It's summer and they're enjoying the cool evening breeze while cuddling with their kids. If we wake even one of them, their brays will alert everyone.

"We have to go to the rear of the property," I whisper to Bruno.

"That's where the house is. You don't think it's crawling with guards back there?"

"No. If there's one thing I know is that Tony Angelo is a fucking idiot. I'd be surprised if there are more than two guards back there. We can take them out."

The second we move out from behind the cover of the oak tree, we begin to take fire. We both drop onto our bellies on the ground next to the wooden fence.

"We're gonna have to crawl to the back of the house. Cover me."

I begin crawling along the edge of the fence, but I don't hear Bruno crawling after me. I don't have to turn my head to know he's been hit. I can't turn my head. Someone can come at me from any direction. But I can't leave Bruno. *Fuck!*

I turn away from the fence and crawl back to Bruno. He's been shot in the clavicle at the base of his neck. There's no tourniquet that can stem the blood gushing from his artery.

I feel around for a pulse on the other side of his neck and it's so weak I can hardly find it. Fucking Bruno.

"You motherfucker," I whisper. "I'll be back for you, buddy. You just sit tight. I'll be back."

I can't get pinned down here. I can't die on the fucking side of a goat farm. And I ain't crawling nowhere.

I stand up and the first bullet whooshes past the right side of my head. I take off running toward the back of the house.

Just sixty yards.

Another bullet takes a chunk out of an oak tree on my right. I keep moving. Faster than I've ever run before.

Ten yards.

Another bullet slices through the wooden fence and shoots a fat splinter of wood straight at my ear.

"Motherfucker!" I cry, but I keep going.

Then I'm there. The back of the house where there are two cars parked in a large dirt lot. The back porch is unguarded. Either this is a trap or I just lucked the fuck out.

I race up the steps and that's when I see Billy laid out on the other side of the porch steps. Dead. A gunshot to the fucking eyeball.

I wrench open the back door with enough force to rip it off its hinges. Where the fuck is John?

I race across the kitchen and into a living room area. He's in the basement. Where's the door to the fucking basement?

It's too dark in here to see shit. I keep bumping into tiny tables. Knocking over lamps and decorative plates. People and their fucking knick knacks.

The gunshot comes without warning and from the space on my right. My eyes begin to adjust a little to the darkness and I see the door to the left of the staircase. It must lead down to the basement.

I pull my .45 out of my waistband and head for the door. I walk slowly at first, but the sounds of moaning urge me on. Please don't let it be John.

Turning the doorknob, I expect gunshots to come immediately, but they don't. I throw open the door and stand to the side, waiting for the shots. Nothing.

Peeking my head around the doorway, I see nothing but a carpeted flight of stairs leading down to more carpet.

I creep down the first few steps slowly, my heart pounding like a fucking jackhammer in my ears. When I reach the second to last step, I see him.

John Veneto lying dead on the carpet not more than eight feet away from me. I take the final step and duck when I see Tony Angelo pointing a gun at me. The shot rips through the drywall above me. The wall coughs up chunks of gypsum all over my head.

"Give it up, Tony. I've got guys all over this place. You're dead."

"Bullshit! Your guys are all dead!"

"You can walk out of here, Tony. All I want is Rebecca. Tell me where she is and we'll let you go."

I press my back against the wall and move my head a little to the left. I think I see a mirror. I inch sideways again and he blows off another shot. This one clips my jacket and leaves the skin on my left arm searing from the heat.

"I've got every reason to kill you!" I shout at him. "Do you know who I am?"

"Do you know who *I* am?"

"Of course I know who you are. You're the low-life cum-dumpster who killed my mother ten years ago."

He laughs at this description. "I like that! Cum-dumpster. Very funny."

"It won't be funny when you're getting cum dumped all over your spleen at Rikers."

"Oh, Jesus fucking Christ. That's hilarious."

This fucking asshole is begging to be shot.

"Enough bullshitting, Tony. Where's Rebecca?"

He finishes his laughing fit. "But you still haven't let me tell you who I am."

"Who the fuck are you?"

"Have you watched Star Wars, Marco?"

My heart drops into my stomach as I realize what he's implying. "You're a fucking liar."

He continues to laugh and that's when I hear it. The same laugh I've heard come out of my own throat for twenty-eight years.

No. There is no fucking way Tony Angelo is my father. This is fucking bullshit!

He won't be my father anymore if I kill him.

But I need to find out where Rebecca is first.

I clutch my hair in desperation. John was my father. Not Tony. And he just killed him. Which means he killed both my mother and father.

I'm gonna kill that motherfucker.

Before I can take the final step down into the basement, the door above me opens and the gunshot hits me square in the chest.

KNOX

volume 4

CASSIA LEO

1

KNOX

THE GUNSHOT FEELS like a sledgehammer to the chest. Her aim is impeccable.

"*FREEZE!* Drop your weapon!" she shouts at me from the top of the basement stairwell.

Both demands are unnecessary. My gun is wedged somewhere underneath my lower back and the wood floor where I'm lying. My shoulders and head are propped up against the wall behind me. I couldn't move if I tried. I feel as if an elephant has stomped on my torso and made bone soup inside my chest cavity.

I can feel the broken ribs piercing my muscle tissue. But that's better than being dead.

The bulletproof vest did its job. And now, injured or not, it's time for me to finish doing mine.

She barrels down the stairs toward me, gun drawn, a steely glare in her eyes, daring me to reach for my gun. She's got a huge set of balls to rush into this basement, but I'd expect nothing less. The first shot out of Tony's gun whizzes past her and lands in the mirror hanging from the wall on my left. I close my eyes and turn my face away from the explosion of glass.

She returns the gunfire, but her aim is much better than his. The gunshot hits Tony's right shoulder, knocking the gun out of his hand. Agent Verduta rushes into the basement, kicking Tony's gun away from him with her thick-soled boot. She proceeds to cuff him as he spits vile insults at her.

Agent Armstrong bounds down the steps toward me, eyes still watery, massive hands clutched around the gun pointed at my head.

I smile at him then turn my attention to Tony. "I'm not done with him," I mutter through the pain as I sit up.

Once I'm standing, Armstrong glances at my gun on the floor, then back at me. He says something about bagging the gun as evidence, but I can't hear over the roaring rush of blood whooshing through my ears. The pain in my chest disappears as my body floods with adrenaline once again.

"*WHERE IS SHE?*" I roar at Tony.

Verduta gently lays him on his back as his blood begins to pool on the dusty wooden floor. I rush further into the basement, but chubby Verduta surprises me with the reflexes of a cat. She draws her gun from her holster and points it at my head when I'm just a few feet away.

"Stay back!" she growls, not an ounce of fear in her eyes. "I don't give a fuck if you're assisting in this investigation. I will blow your *fucking* head off!"

We stare each other down for a moment. The air is completely still, charged with electricity. My muscles are wound so taut I can hardly breathe. I can sense Armstrong's huge presence somewhere behind me. No doubt his gun is pointed at the back of my skull.

I grit my teeth, trying to temper the desperation. I need to find Rebecca. That was the whole *fucking* deal! If I gave them Tony, they'd let me question him. But I'm sure Verduta knew the moment Tony dropped the bomb that he's my biological father, she couldn't leave me alone with him in this basement.

She was right. If she hadn't shot me, I was going to kill him. Even despite the deal I made with Geneva.

I offered to let Tony live if Geneva promised to keep what happened in that warehouse, and my true identity, a secret. Pregnant women are not easy to negotiate with; especially when you've just murdered the father of their child. But her silence in exchange for her father's life was a small compromise to make.

And now that I know the truth about Tony Angelo's identity, I'm sickened by another realization. By killing

Nico, I killed my unborn nephew's father. This thought only makes me want to kill Tony even more. If I don't do something soon, I'll explode with hatred.

"*WHERE THE FUCK IS SHE?*" I demand.

Tony coughs then lets out a weak cackle. "She's dead."

He continues to laugh. Verduta keeps her gun trained on my forehead as my fists clench at my sides.

"He's full of shit, Savage," Verduta tries to reassure me. "You know it and I know it. Don't fall for this. Don't do something you'll regret. Think of Rebecca."

"She's suckin' on seawater!" Tony cackles. "Bye-bye, Rebecca."

Verduta can sense my patience waning as my adrenaline peaks. The lion in me is ready to pounce. Just when I'm certain she's going to pull the trigger and blow my head off, she spins away from me and pistol-whips Tony.

He's out.

She spins around and points her weapon at me again. "Don't even fucking think about it. He can't answer any more of your burning questions, so I suggest you get the fuck out of here."

I shake my head, unable to believe that this could have gone so fucking wrong.

"You said I could talk to him. That was the whole fucking deal!"

"It's too late. Deal with it."

Armstrong steps between Verduta and me, ready to tackle me if I make another move.

John is dead. Billy is dead. Bruno is probably dead. I'm not any closer to knowing where Rebecca is. And even if I do find her, I don't know if she's alive. And even if she's alive, I'll have to tell her that her father is dead.

Turning away from Verduta, I look at John, where he lies about eight feet away from Tony. I close my eyes as I take a step toward him and wait for someone to shoot.

2

KNOX

NEITHER VERDUTA OR Armstrong discharge their weapons. I fall to my knees next to John, turning him onto his back so I can see his face.

His skin is pale from the loss of blood. Tony must have ambushed him from behind when he entered the basement. The gunshot entered at the base of John's skull and there's no exit wound. The bottom half of his jaw and his neck are covered in blood. His eyes are wide with shock.

I push his eyelids shut and close my eyes. Rebecca's face materializes through the red cast on the backs of my eyelids. I clench my jaw as I take deep breaths.

"Sorry, John. I fucked up. But I won't let you down again."

My mind draws back to a hot summer day in Bensonhurst when I was seventeen. I'd been hustling for John for two months. He didn't want me involved in any of his business. He promised my mom he'd never let me do anything illegal. But I was a persistent little shit.

Jerry Mainella and I enter the shop through the rear entrance, as usual. We head straight through the kitchen and into the dining area. The first booth on the left is John's booth. And, as usual, he's sitting there with Frank and Tony. They're eating antipasti and sipping Peroni while John sips limonata.

"Come. Sit," John orders us as he scoots over and nods toward the empty spot on his right.

I take a seat next to him as Jerry pulls up a chair from a neighboring table.

"We were just discussing how you boys are gonna stop hustling when school starts."

I look at John, ready to protest this decision, but the stern look on his face tells me I'll get nowhere with him on this subject. His mind is made up.

"I can still work weekends. You don't gotta pay me," I insist, grabbing a bocconcini off the tray and popping it in my mouth.

He laughs at this suggestion, but I'm dead serious. It's not the extra pocket money that made me want to work for John. It's the power.

When people know you work for John Veneto, they

treat you differently. Walk into a room and people fall all over themselves trying to accommodate you. At school, even the teachers treat me differently. I cut class two days in a row last week and never got detention. Being known as one of John's soldiers is a rush you can't put a price on.

"Look at this kid," John says, putting his arm around my shoulders and giving me a good shake. "He don't wanna get paid. He does it for the love."

Just as he says this, Rebecca walks in the front door of the restaurant and heads straight for our booth. John continues to brag to Tony and Frank about what a good kid I am and I try not to look too pleased with myself. Jerry sometimes gets jealous and makes fun of me. Calls me "Johnny's pet."

But I don't know what Jerry's thinking or doing right now because all I can see is Rebecca. Every step she takes, her silky brown hair bounces on her bare shoulders. She's wearing a blue tube top and tiny cutoff jean shorts. Her pink lipgloss makes her mouth glimmer in the dull restaurant lighting. Everything about her shines. She's beautiful.

I lower my head and stare at the surface of the wooden table to keep from looking at her again.

John leans in and whispers in my ear, "Don't get any crazy ideas. She's too young for you." I swallow hard and nod my head. He laughs as he squeezes my shoulder. "Good things come to those who wait.... They also get to keep their legs."

This makes me laugh and gives me the courage to look up as Rebecca arrives at our table. Jerry looks away, the same way I did just a moment ago. Then she smiles at me.

That's all it takes. One dazzling smile. And right there I make a promise to myself: I'll wait for Rebecca. As long as it takes.

I open my eyes and someone's standing over John and me. A crime scene tech. He's waiting for me to move so he can collect his evidence. Then the coroner can come in, bag John up and take him away. The pain in my chest returns, but this ache has nothing to do with the gunshot.

I haven't made many promises in my life. I don't believe in making promises I may not deliver on. But I know I'll find Rebecca. And when I do, I'll keep the promise I made to John when I asked for Rebecca's hand in marriage. I promised him I'd keep her safe for at least two years before I marry her.

"I'll wait at least two years," I whisper to John. "I'll wait as long as it takes."

3

KNOX

THE MEDIC WON'T let me leave unless I allow her to bandage my ribs. I try insisting that I'm fine. I've broken more ribs than a crash test dummy. But she's not impressed with this information.

I sit on the gurney with my shirt off as she wraps the adhesive bandage across my chest, under my left arm and over my right shoulder. All I can think of as her fingers whisper over my skin is Rebecca. I stare at the flashing lights on top of the ambulance next to us. Anything not to look at her as she touches me. Finally, she finishes bandaging me up and I hop off the gurney and mutter my thanks as I walk away.

I stop by Verduta and Armstrong's car to update them on my plans. Verduta still looks annoyed. The woman shoots me in the chest and she has the nerve to be annoyed with me. If that rat bastard Tony would have given up Rebecca's location I wouldn't have charged her in the basement. Not that I thought Tony would just give up the information. But I expected to have more time to get it out of him.

"I'm flying out in twenty. I need to tell Marie myself."

Armstrong nods his head and Verduta shrugs. "Not like we can stop you, right?"

"You're a fast learner, Karen."

She winces at the use of her first name. "Don't ever call me Karen again."

I slap the hood of the blue Crown Victoria. "As long as you all don't send any units to Marie's until morning. It'll be past midnight by the time I get there to break the news. She needs some time to process everything and get some rest. That's all I'm asking."

Verduta heaves a long sigh and shakes her head. "Eight a.m. tomorrow. She better be ready to talk. We still have two missing persons on our hands." She glances around at the flurry of cops, detectives, and medics. "And don't go trying to find them on your own. That's our job, remember?"

I smile and nod because I know that last line was just for show. Verduta knows if there's anyone who'll find Rebecca, it's me. And that's exactly what I'm going to do. But first I have to tell Marie her husband is dead.

Shortly after finding out Bruno was transported to the hospital, just barely holding on, the helicopter arrives in a large field behind the farmhouse. I keep my chin down as I approach the chopper, then I pull myself in and breathe a sigh of relief. August is sitting there, his head in his hands as he leans forward.

"Relax," I say, taking a seat next to him. "That was excellent timing on the FBI tip."

I was going to kill August after he confessed his love for Rebecca to me a few days ago. Instead, I decided I could make August's confused feelings work to my advantage. Besides, I didn't think killing August would win me any favors with Rebecca. It may have even turned August into a martyr in her eyes, and I couldn't have that.

August finally sits up and glances at me as he leans back. "They wanted to know why I'm working with you."

"What did you tell them?"

"I told them what you told me to say: I can't stand by and watch while you fuck this up. Someone has to make sure Rebecca's found."

I let out a hearty laugh and August smiles. "You little albino cocksucker. You always know what to say to bust my gut."

His smile disappears. "What if you don't find her?"

"I'll find her."

"You have to at least consider the possibility. What are you going to tell—"

"I'll *find* her!"

He turns away to look down at the city lights as we fly over Claremont. I take a deep breath to calm myself before I throw him out of the fucking helicopter. Then I lean back and shake my head.

Ten years. I've spent the last ten years modeling my life into a fishing net built to catch one big fish. Staking everything I had on my ability to lure in Tony so I could show him as much mercy as he showed my mother. I finally have him where I want him and what do I do? I throw away the last ten years for a woman.

Not even for a woman, because Rebecca's not sitting next to me right now. I threw away my ten-year vendetta for the mere chance of seeing Rebecca again.

Losing a loved one will make you do crazy things. But falling in love with someone will make you completely insane.

"Your uncle is being transported to Connecticut tomorrow."

August turns to me, his blonde eyebrow cocked in disbelief. "Is this another lie? Am I going to have to kill my mother or rip out my own beating heart and hand it over first? What's the catch?"

I shake my head at his grandeur. "There no fucking catch. I said I'd bring your crook of an uncle back into the country if you did this for me and that's exactly what I did. I'm a man of my word."

He nods as he looks out the window again. "Why does it still feel like I lost?"

"Because you're a cheating piece of shit, just like your Uncle Stewart. You never should have taken that girl up to your apartment August." I smile as he clenches his fist, but he doesn't look at me. "I've been waiting for Rebecca for eleven years. This was never going to be a fair fight."

The helicopter touches down on the rooftop of Knox Security a quarter to midnight. I look at August and he looks scared as a teenage girl in a men's locker room.

"Buck up, August. It's time for phase two."

"What's phase two?"

"Phase two is where I bring Rebecca home and you look for a new girlfriend."

4

KNOX

THE CAR PULLS up to the two-story house on the corner of 80th Street and 19th Avenue and my gut clenches inside me. There aren't many things that make me nervous. But knocking on Marie's door at six minutes past midnight makes me feel like a fucking juvenile delinquent.

For some reason, I'm not at all surprised when Marie answers the door within minutes. As if she were sitting in the kitchen waiting for someone to knock on her door. She takes one look at my shirt, stained with Bruno and John's blood, and the tears come fast.

I catch her in my arms before she can collapse. Holding her tightly against me, I can't help but think of my mother. She would also be devastated to learn of John's death. At least that's one less heart I'll have to break tonight.

Maintaining my hold on her, I close the front door and lead her into the dimly lit living room. I sit down on the brown leather sofa where John probably used to cheer on the Yankees. I squat down in front of her so my bloody clothes don't soil her furniture, then I grab her hand.

"I'm sorry, Marie. I tried to protect him, but you know John. He likes to do stuff on his own. He doesn't take orders from anyone."

She stares at her lap where my hand envelops hers. The tears stream down her face as she silently contemplates this news. Finally, she squeezes my hand and looks up at me.

"I've imagined this day a million times, but I never imagined you'd be the one holding my hand." She wipes her cheeks and takes a deep breath. "I don't think either of us will be sleeping tonight. Come have an espresso with me. I want to hear all your best stories about John."

I sit at the breakfast table in her pristine white kitchen while she prepares us both an espresso. By the time she arrives at the table with our drinks and takes a seat next to me, there's not a trace of moisture around her eyes. Just like Rebecca when she came back into my life last month. Unwilling to crumble until I showed her how good it felt to let go.

"John took me to Henry's chop shop when I was sixteen," I begin and she shakes her head in dismay. "Wait, it gets better."

"I'm sure it does. Go on."

I take a sip of my espresso, taking a moment to breathe in the warm earth aroma, then I continue. "I had just gotten my driver's license and I was desperate for a car of my own. My ma couldn't afford to get me a car and she was always working." I glance at her to see if she's getting uncomfortable with me talking about my mom, but she just stares at the table. "Anyway, I was itching to start hustling for John."

"I thought this story was gonna get better," Marie teases me.

I chuckle then I continue telling her the story of how John helped me get my first legit car—a '67 Ford Mustang. I spent every night and every weekend in my garage working on that car for four months until it purred like a kitten. All he wanted in return was to be the first person I took for a ride in that baby.

This story gives Marie pause. She stares at the tiny espresso cup in her hands for a moment, digesting the story of this simple gesture of kindness. As if she's trying to reconcile the John in my story with the brutal John Veneto we see portrayed on the news or the philandering husband she's loved since she was a teenager.

"You never really know someone, you know?" She wears a weak smile as she slowly spins the espresso cup in her hands. "I thought I knew the kind of bastard he could be. But it wasn't until he thought he was going to prison for the rest of his life that I finally began to see the John I fell in love with twenty-nine years ago. The kid who walked me home every day after school and waited until I was seventeen before he asked me out. Who the hell was I married to all these years? Because it wasn't that kid and it sure as hell wasn't the man who got you your first car."

"Marie, we all make mistakes. The important thing is that he loved you."

"Love is not enough, Marco. Love is just a feeling. It only means something when it's acted upon. And John had a real sick way of loving me." She turns and looks me in the eye. "Don't make the same mistakes we made. Don't hurt my little girl."

"I would never. And I'm going to find her, Marie. I won't stop looking until she's home safe."

She closes her eyes and grabs the bridge of her nose, pressing her fingers into the corners of her eyes. Then she lets out a soft whimper and finally lets go. I sit with her a while longer while she weeps and shares a few stories with me. All the stories are about her and John when they were kids, but the last story is about me.

"I can't believe I forgot to tell you this the last time you came here. A few years after Ella died, maybe four or five years, Lori Franco thought she saw someone who looked like you snooping around your old house. I told Johnny and he said it couldn't have been you because you were living in some other country and you didn't want nothing to do with that place. Was it you?"

I think back to the last time I snuck into Bensonhurst. It was five years ago. I'd been all over the world building connections as I started up Knox Security. It was my first night back in New York and I couldn't help myself. I had to get a look at the old house. I wanted to know if the people who lived there looked happy. I wanted to know that it was possible for someone to still be happy in that house.

I had a crazy superstitious belief that if I looked through their window and saw a family watching TV together or having dinner together, that it would mean I had to give up my vendetta. Because my mother's ghost was gone. She was at peace. I could let her go and move on.

But I looked through the window into that family's living room and all I saw was a young teenage girl sitting on a sofa. She was hugging her knees to her chest and crying. She didn't look anything like Rebecca, but I thought of Rebecca when I saw her. Then I thought of John and what he'd done to Frank Mainella. He wouldn't want me to quit. He wanted Tony dead as much as I did.

"Yeah, that was me," I say, swallowing the knot in my throat.

"That place got foreclosed on almost two years ago and nobody's been in there since," Marie continues as she gathers our espresso cups. "But I saw a couple of guys around there yesterday and I figured it was a couple of your guys."

"You saw some guys around there yesterday?"

Her eyebrows knit in confusion. "They weren't your guys?"

"Fuck!" Her eyes widen with fright. "I'm sorry, Marie. I didn't mean to scare you. I just—I should have fuckin' known!"

"You think… you think they have Rebecca there?"

I shake my head, trying to temper this insane hope churning inside me. "I don't know. But I'm about to find out."

I shoot up from my chair and head for the door with Marie on my heels. "Shouldn't you get some backup or something? You can't go there alone."

"I've got one of my guys outside." I turn around to face her when I reach the door. "Stay here. Don't answer the phone and don't answer the door for anyone. You got it?"

She nods and though I can see she's worried sick, there's a trace of hope gleaming in her eyes, as well. "Be careful."

"I will."

"And, Marco?"

"Yeah?"

"Don't show them any mercy."

"I won't."

5

REBECCA

THEY'RE MOVING US. Finally!

It took a little scheming on our part, and a couple of days of starvation, but Lita and I finally got them to move us out of this basement. Yesterday, we wrapped our breakfast of toast and eggs in large wads of toilet tissue and stuffed them into the toilet until it was completely stopped up. Then we slid our plates back through the flap in the door, empty and covered in blood-soaked tissue. The blood was actually from my finger. But it got their attention.

We finally heard one of our captors' voices when the jerk came to pick up our plates and yelled, "What the fuck?" We screamed at him that we were both menstruating and the toilet was stopped up. We didn't hear anything from any of them the rest of yesterday, and all day today.

We were beginning to think we'd made a grievous error, until they slipped a typed note, two silk hoods, and two pairs of handcuffs through the slot in the door. The note says to put our shoes on, then cuff one of our hands to the drain under the sink and use the other hand to put the hood over our head. They're moving us tonight. Which means our plan worked!

They're giving us ten minutes to get cuffed and ready for them to come down. This is the moment we've been waiting for. This is our chance to make a run for it.

Lita's gray eyes are dulled by the lack of food. She doesn't usually skip meals. She usually eats six small meals per day. Her biological mother has diabetes and she insists that small regular meals will prevent her from getting it. Nevertheless, five days in a basement eating two to three large meals full of starch has given Lita major heartburn and deadly flatulence. Which has been a source of both tears and laughter for us in our basement prison.

"So you're going to pretend to pass out from low blood sugar," Lita whispers as we both sit on the wood floor beneath the utility sink and cuff ourselves to the drainpipe.

She's the one with the family history of diabetes, but I'm the one who's going to pretend to pass out. Not that we think they know anything about our family medical history. But I agreed to be the one who fake-faints because I'm the one who took an acting class at Hunter College. Something I'm seriously regretting right now.

"What if they don't care that I passed out? Or what if they try to force-feed me some candy or something?"

"Then we'll go to Plan B."

"Which is…?"

"Scratch, claw, punch, and scream."

I haven't told Lita about the possibility that I might be pregnant. It just seems so unlikely with Knox's history; vasectomy reversals don't always go well. And I don't want to see the pity or relief in Lita's eyes if we find out later that I'm not pregnant. Because, yes, it will be disappointing. No matter how hard I've tried not to think about what it would be like to have a child with Knox, I've had nothing but time to think about that for the past five days.

But time is running out. They'll be down to retrieve us any minute now. I don't have time to tell Lita all the details right now. But she needs to know why I can't do what she just suggested.

"I can't do Plan B. I might be pregnant."

Her mouth drops open. "Oh, my God. Why didn't you tell me earlier?"

"Like I said. I *might* be pregnant. I don't know for sure yet."

"You need to eat something. We never should have

antagonized them.”

“You didn’t know they were going to withhold our food.”

“I’m so sorry. How are you feeling?” She uses her free hand to brush my grimy hair out of my face and something about this gesture gets me all emotional.

“Honestly, I do feel like I’m going to pass out any second here.” I grab my black silk hood and nod at the hood in her lap. “We have to put these on. They’ll be down here soon.”

We give each other a one-armed hug before we pull our hoods over our heads. My heart is thrumming loudly in my ears and pulsing in my fingertips. I’ve tried to stay hydrated since they stopped feeding us yesterday, but I feel lethargic and light-headed. I couldn’t fight off these guys; not even if they were the ones cuffed and blindfolded.

“I love you, Lita. Even if you were scheming to break up August and me for the past seven months.”

She chuckles, but I hear a trace of a whimper. “I love you, Rebecca. Even if you have terrible taste in men.”

The creak of the basement door swinging open makes me freeze. I can’t see anything through the black fabric, except the crack of light at the base of the hood where it rests on my chest. As soon as I hear the first footstep fall onto the wooden staircase, all I can hear is the thunderous pounding of my heartbeat. My entire body begins to shake as adrenaline is dumped into my bloodstream. My fingers get cold and numb as the blood rushes away from my extremities back to my vital organs.

My last thought before I pass out is that I don't need to pretend anymore.

6

KNOX

DAVE MACMILLAN DROVE me to Marie's tonight. Dave has only completed a few jobs with me. He's a good guy. He came highly recommended from my top security adviser. He was Special Ops in Iraq for a few years before he took a private security job in Saudi Arabia. He's a sharp shooter and his reflexes are better than Bruno's and Billy's, but he's a hothead. He tends to act without thinking. With Billy dead and Bruno clinging to life in a Vermont hospital, Dave is my best alternative. I hope he doesn't fuck this up for me.

"It's one story with a basement. You approach from the front and sweep the first floor. I'm approaching from the alley. That's most likely where they're coming in and out. They may be hiding out in the garage or the shed."

We load up our holsters and pack some more ammunition in our pockets. I didn't come prepared for this. No bulletproof vest this time. "Then we'll rendezvous in the kitchen and you cover me as I go into the basement. Got it?"

He nods and the gleam in his eyes makes me a little nervous. It's been too long since he's been on one of these missions. He's thirsty for blood.

We split up at the corner and I motion toward the alley to let him know I'm moving on. He continues down the street toward the house where I grew up. The place where it all began.

I get to the rear fence of the house on the corner and peek my head into the alley. The back of a white van is sticking halfway out of my old garage. The same garage where I brought to life a '67 Mustang.

Either that's a very long white van or these guys are headed out soon. As this thought crosses my mind, a big guy in dark clothing and a white knit cap appears at the back of the van. His hand is locked around the arm of a hooded figure. A female. She's barefoot and thin, but way too tall to be Rebecca. It must be Lita.

She doesn't fight him until he shoves her into the back of the van. Her long, thin legs flail out, trying to kick the guy as he walks away. He doesn't pay her any attention as he disappears around the other side of the van.

My heart pounds as I anticipate where he went. Is

Rebecca already inside that van or did he just go to retrieve her? My question is answered seconds later when the guy in the cap arrives at the back of the van. He's carrying the limp body of a woman. Though she appears to be dead, her hands are still cuffed in front of her and her head is covered in a black hood.

It's her.

My veins floods with pure madness and wild determination. I'm going to kill every last one of these motherfuckers.

My vision becomes more focused as my hearing is trained on every movement the guy in the cap makes. He sets Rebecca down in the back of the van and slams the doors shut. I wait for him to step away from the van, then I fire.

The shot sounds like a soft pop through my silencer. It won't wake anyone in this alley. And the shot to the head sure put him to sleep. But this alley is bound to be crawling with goons in a matter of seconds.

Exactly what I'm hoping for.

The first one arrives to check on his buddy and I take a clean shot at the hand that holds his weapon. His gun skids across the pavement in the alley and the guy looks straight at me. From where I'm standing just thirty yards away, I smile then I pull the trigger once more and he falls slumped over his friend.

I don't know what's going on inside the house with

Dave. But I'm guessing that most of these guys are already outside if they were planning on moving Rebecca and Lita tonight. They probably heard of Tony's downfall in Vermont and now they're enacting a new plan.

I see the muzzle of the gun first as it peeks around the corner of the garage, then a corner of the guy's head. He needs to come out further if he wants to take a shot at me.

"I'm right here, motherfucker! Take your best shot!"

He steps out at the same time another guy steps out from behind the van. I take out the guy behind the van in one shot, but the other guy gets a shot off. It whizzes past my neck and gets my heart racing, but my next shot hits him in the chest.

Four guys. Could there be more?

As if I've asked this question to the heavens, I get a response a second later. "All clear! I'm coming out!"

It's Dave's voice. He steps into the alley and my muscles relax a little. He doesn't appear to be shot. Not that I expected him to be. His aim is better than mine.

I race toward the garage, my chest ready to burst with a mixture of relief and worry. I'm finally going to see Rebecca. This five-day nightmare is almost over. Unless her limp body was an indication that I arrived too late.

I'm ten yards from the garage when the van backs up so fast, the tires squeal against the pavement. Whoever's in the driver's seat shifts into drive and takes off past Dave and down the alley away from me. Dave raises his gun and shoots at the driver's side, but he hits the back window instead.

"Stop!" I roar at him. "Rebecca is in there, you dumbfuck!"

His eyes are narrowed as I approach him, still staring at the end of the alley where the white van got away. "Sorry, boss."

I could rip this asshole to shreds right now. "Just get in the fucking car!"

I nod toward a sporty Cadillac STS that was parked next to the white van in the garage. It's running with the keys in the ignition. Dave slides into the driver's seat and peels out of the garage and down the alley after the van.

We catch up to the van on 65th Street. Then he heads straight onto the expressway. He's headed for the bridge.

Good, he'll have a tough time getting away when he hits the one a.m. pedestrian traffic in Chinatown. Once he's on the expressway, he guns it and we stay on his tail at ninety miles-per-hour. He swerves to avoid the occasional car, but we never lose him.

Dave speeds up a bit until he's almost on the van's bumper. I point my gun at him and he slows down to put a safer distance between us and the van. I shouldn't have to tell Dave how fucking important it is that we hang back. At this speed, a small tap on the bumper will send the van careening across the expressway.

I keep hoping that he'll slow down to take one of the

exits, or that we'll hit some traffic, but neither happens. My stomach and jaw are clenched, waiting for him to get to the bridge. He'll have to slow down at least a little when he hits the bridge.

Six minutes later, he slows down to sixty-five and gets into the right lane to take the bridge exit.

"Now?" Dave asks.

"Not yet. Let them get on the bridge first."

The van slows down even more to take the curve on the exit ramp. When the curve ends, Dave glances at me.

"Not yet. The guardrail is only a few feet high here."

As soon as I say this, the van speeds up to get onto the bridge and Dave speeds up. As soon as we pass the green and white sign for FDR Drive, and the metal railing encloses us on all sides like a cage, I give Dave the green light.

"Pull up on his left."

Dave pulls into the left lane and speeds up a little so I can take out the left rear tire before he can speed up any more. The van swerves a little. The tire shreds and flies off, but it only slows him down a little. I nod my head and Dave takes us over to the other side and I shoot out the other rear tire. This causes him to lose control and the van slides into the guardrail on the right side of the bridge.

The driver's side door and the back door fly open at the same time. I don't know where to look as Dave stops the car next to the disabled van. The skinny guy that jumps out of the van races across the bridge, nearly getting run over by a taxi that's trying to pass us up.

I raise my gun and point it at him as he rushes toward the pedestrian bridge. I'm about to squeeze the trigger when I hear the sweetest sound I've ever heard.

"Knox?"

I turn toward the back of the van and Lita is helping Rebecca out of the trunk. I drop my gun and race to her. If there's one thing I've learned over the past five days it's that love always trumps vengeance.

I wrap my arms around her and lift her out of the van. She holds onto my neck, but I can feel the weakness in her embrace.

"My princess." I kiss her temple and squeeze her gently. "Baby, are you okay? Did they hurt you?"

"No," she whispers hoarsely. "But I could really go for a slice of pizza right now."

I pull my head back to look her in the eye. Her brown eyes are a bit sunken in, but they're still burning with that fire they always get when she's near me. She's telling me the truth.

"I'll get you anything you want." I kiss her forehead and her lips hint at a smile. "But first I have one thing to do."

I set her down on the bridge as the soft sound of sirens rises in the distance. Then I kneel down on one knee and take her left hand in mine. I plant a soft kiss on her knuckles and she covers her mouth with her other hand.

"Rebecca Veneto: I love you." I take a deep breath, keeping my gaze trained on her eyes so I don't lose my grasp on this shred of certainty. "I've never said those words to any woman other than my ma. But they've never been more true.

"For ten years, you were the girl of my dreams. Losing you five days ago was the beginning of my nightmare. I've been chasing my tail trying to track you down. You drive me crazy." She smiles down at me and I swallow hard. "The past few days without you have made me sick. I don't ever want be without you again. I want you next to me, safe, for the rest of my life. Will you marry me... in two to three years?"

She laughs out loud at this. I don't know if the tears streaming down her face are a good or bad sign, but my stomach is in knots waiting for her to say something. Then she nods and I feel as if I could fly to the moon.

"Yes!" she says brightly. "Yes, I'll marry you. I'll marry you in two years, three years, or a hundred years. Yes!"

She falls to her knees and I kiss her for the first time in five days. And for the first time in ten years, I'm free.

7

REBECCA

THE QUESTION AND answer session at the 7th Precinct in the Lower East Side is short. Lita and I are questioned separately, but our lack of injuries corroborates our story that we were not assaulted while in captivity.

They question Knox and Dave about what happened at Marco's old house and they have expert answers. They're just Good Samaritans who stumbled upon a crime in progress. Lita and I appeared to be in "imminent peril." They defended themselves while trying to protect Lita and I from further injury.

We leave the 7th Precinct at 3:40 a.m., getting a glimpse of the van's driver in another interrogation room on the way out. Our police escort drops Lita off at her apartment first.

"Call me when you wake up. You owe me brunch," Lita says as she leans over and kisses my cheek.

"You're the one who stood me up," I tease her.

She shakes her head as she slides out of the back of the police car, then pokes her head back inside. "And don't forget to tell me about *you-know-what?*"

She slams the car door shut and drags herself up the front steps of her apartment building. I glance at Knox to see if he knows what she was referring to and he's wearing that cunning half-smile. I can't hide anything from this man.

Officer Helms drops us off at Knox's apartment. Despite his injuries, Knox insists on carrying me up the front steps and the staircase to the second floor master bathroom. I can see him gritting his teeth against the pain, but he refuses to let me go.

We take a long, luxurious shower together. Washing away every bit of the last five days. I'm careful when I scrub the right side of his chest where he took a bullet to his vest.

"Whose blood is this?" I ask as I scrub a bit of caked blood off his forearm.

His gaze falls to the floor and my stomach aches as I wait for him to respond. "Your father didn't make it out."

My entire body gets weak and Knox catches me around the waist before I collapse. I fall into his arms and he holds me tightly against him as I cry.

I know my father wasn't a great man. Maybe he wasn't even a good man. But I loved him. And I know everything he did was to protect my mother and me—and Marco. To provide us with the best and to deliver us the justice he believed we deserved.

And now I'll never be able to tell him that I forgive him. I forgive him for what he did to Frank Mainella. I forgive him for loving two women at once. I forgive him for not knowing that I've needed him every day for the last four years we were apart.

Once we're out of the shower, Knox dries me off and helps me get dressed. Then he forces me to eat some crackers and juice before we go to bed.

We lie facing each other in the darkness. He reaches up and lays his warm hand on the side of my face. Then he softly brushes his thumb across my cheek.

"He wanted to get you back himself," he whispers. "He couldn't sit back and watch."

I heave a long, stuttered sigh and nod.

He kisses my forehead. "Go to sleep, princess."

"Knox?"

"Yes?"

I place my hand lightly over the right side of his chest. "Thank you."

"You don't have to thank me."

"Thank you for loving my father."

He's silent for a moment and I feel as if I've broken

down the final blocks of stone around his heart. I clasp my hand around the back of his neck and pull his lips to mine. His warm hand lands on my hip and he begins to roll me onto my back. I press my hand against the left side of his chest and push him back.

"You lay back. You're injured."

He hesitates for a moment, unsure whether he's willing to relinquish control. Then he lies back for me. I run my fingertips over his solid chest, then down his smooth abs. I reach the light trail of hair under his navel and his skin prickles.

"I love you," I whisper as I wrap my fingers around his hard length.

He sucks in a sharp breath and pulls me closer so my chest is on top of his. "I love you more." He grabs my face and kisses me slowly. "I'll always love you more."

I climb on top of him and gasp into his mouth as he enters me. His hands are warm as they glide over my back and down to my butt. He grabs hold of me and pushes my hips down as his hips thrust upward. I cry out in pain as he hits my cervix.

"Are you okay?"

"Yes," I reply quickly, though a tiny voice in my head is telling me that this is a sign. Maybe I *am* pregnant. "Don't stop."

I clench myself around his cock as we thrust in unison. Each time we connect so deep it sends a bolt of pain through my core. My nipples rub against his chest as we move together. He keeps one hand on my waist and the other tangled in my hair as he kisses me. I grind into him slowly, savoring the friction of my clit against his pelvic bone. My breathing quickly turns to panting and my whimpers turn to screams.

"I want you to have my babies." He groans as he comes and attempts to thrust even deeper.

I let out a soft chuckle. "Babies? With an *S*?"

"We're gonna do this all day, every day," he says, his waning erection twitches inside me, "until there's an army of Savage children running around this house."

"Savage children," I whisper, then I lick the clean sweat at the base of his neck, smiling when his cock jumps. "Sounds ominous."

And then he's hard again. He wasn't kidding about all day, every day.

8

REBECCA

KNOX INSISTS ON taking me to his private doctor as soon
as we wake up at eleven. His doctor has a private office
inside Knox Security. Maintaining the health of his
employees is very important to Knox.

Once my blood is drawn, we're taken into a very
modern and cold examination room to wait for the doctor.
Knox and I stand next to the examination table as he
holds my trembling hand.

"It's so cold in here."

"You don't have to be nervous."

"I'm not nervous," I reply too quickly.

He wraps his arms around my shoulders and pulls me
against him. I bury my face in his warm chest and breathe
in his scent. All it takes is a few deep breaths and the

trembling subsides.

He kisses the top of my head and loosens his hold on me. "It's okay if you're not pregnant now. We've got plenty of time. I promised your dad I'd wait to marry you until I've kept you safe at least two years."

"That's what you meant when you asked if I'd marry you in two to three years?"

He grins and plants a quick kiss on my cheek. "I always keep my promises. I promise you we're going to have lots of babies."

The door swings open and the doctor enters with her eyes cast downward, looking at the tablet resting in the crook of her arm. Dr. Inglehoffer is a woman. Dr. Inglehoffer is an attractive woman. Probably early forties, and I must admit that the thought of her giving Knox any type of exam makes me crazy jealous. The sides of her silky brown hair are pulled back in a knot at the back of her head. Her red-rimmed glasses are stylish, even sitting atop the end of her nose as she reads the results of the blood test.

She looks up from the tablet and smiles at me. "You're four weeks pregnant."

Knox's hand tightens around mine. When I look up at him, his eyes are closed.

"I'll give you two a moment," Inglehoffer says as she quietly leaves the examination room.

The door closes softly behind her. My heart pounds as

I wait for Knox to say something. Then his gorgeous lips curl up into that sexy grin I love so much. His eyelids open slowly and there's a carnal hunger in his eyes. Like a lion who's cornered his prey.

I bite my lip as I anticipate his next move. Then in one swift motion, he positions himself in front of me, where I sit on the examination table. He spreads my knees apart, then his hand slides under my skirt and into my panties as his mouth locks on mine.

"Knox!" I protest into his mouth. "There are people outside!"

"I don't give a fuck. This is *my* building." He takes a step back and yanks my panties down. "All mine."

His face disappears beneath the gray silk fabric of my skirt. His fingers part my flesh as his mouth closes around my clit. My muscles tense and twitch as he sucks gently. Then he moves down and thrusts his tongue inside me.

"Oh, God."

A chuckle issues from deep inside his chest. "You taste different today."

"What?"

"Sweeter."

I relax at this clarification, then I lie back and close my eyes as he devours me. He consumes slowly, teasing and hinting at a spectacular finish, until I have to beg him to make me come. When he's done, he gives me a moment to regain my strength before he bends me over the examination table.

My bare ass is in the air, my elbows resting on the cushioned table, as a knock at the door startles me. Knox continues thrusting into me, completely undaunted.

"She's coming in!" I whisper urgently.

He chuckles softly, but doesn't answer me. Almost as if he wants to get caught.

"Knox!" I cry as the doorknob begins to turn and the door is pushed open an inch.

"We're busy!" he roars and the door slams shut.

"Jesus Christ!"

He laughs as he continues piercing me, faster now. His sac nudges my hard nub with each thrust and soon I'm getting closer to another orgasm. He reaches around and massages my clit as his other arm tightens around my waist.

"You like that, princess?" His mouth is hot on my neck as his cock stretches me slowly one moment then rams into me the next.

"Yes," I murmur.

"Come for me," he growls into my ear as he caresses my clit. "Come all over me."

I whimper as my body twitches and my knees turn to rubber. My arms tremble and give out beneath me. The side of my face presses against the cool paper covering the exam table as my eyes roll back into my head. My pussy clenches around his cock as I come hard.

He finishes a minute later and collapses on top of me. "I love you so fucking much," he breathes into my ear.

He pulls out of me and I get that familiar empty feeling I despise so much. If there's one thing I'm certain of, it's that Knox and I were made to fit together like two shiny cogs in a machine. When we're apart, everything stops turning.

He stands up and turns me around to face him. "Do you know what it means to be a partner?"

"Of course."

"My mom told me something shortly before she died. She said women don't want to be owned. They want a partner. An equal part of a whole." I smile because this is not at all what I would expect from Knox after what we just did. "I always thought she was full of shit, but now I get it. Before you, I was half the man I was meant to be. Without you there is no me."

I wrap my arms and legs around him as he lifts me off the floor. Then I breathe in the crisp scent of his skin. The scent of forever.

EPILOGUE

six years later

9

KNOX

I WAKE TO find myself alone in bed. A beam of white light is shining through the crack in the curtains, cutting the bed in half. My half and hers. I prop myself up on my elbows to look around for signs of her, but there's no pile of discarded clothing or anything. Then the bathroom door opens and there she is, in all her naked glory, hair still damp from the shower.

She smiles as she glides toward the bed. "Good morning."

My gaze follows her body, taking in the soft curves of her hips and the fullness of her breasts. She never looks sexier than when she's pregnant. Which is probably why she's pregnant for the fourth time in six years.

She climbs onto the bed with a sly twinkle in her eye. I

grab her waist and she squeals as I throw her down onto her back.

"I can smell that pineapple lotion," I growl, burying my face in her neck.

She knows that lotion drives me crazy. I slip my hand between her thighs and she gladly spreads her legs for me. Her clit is hard and ready to be touched. I slide my finger into her pussy to gather her wetness first, then I caress her clit in tight circles right over the one o'clock position where she's most sensitive.

I kiss her neck and get a hint of the pineapple flavor. Removing my hand from between her legs, I slide my finger into my mouth. As I suspected: sweet, succulent pineapple.

"You're such a cheater," I whisper into her ear and she laughs.

I kiss my way down her shoulder, over her chest, licking the smooth skin over her belly as I continue. She lets out a soft squeak as I take her clit into my mouth. The taste of her alone is better than the lotion, but something about her trying to make herself more edible is a huge turn-on.

I spread her flesh apart and lay a soft kiss on her clit. It's such a tiny thing, but it's mine. Like the tiny person growing inside her.

I lick her lightly because I know it drives her crazy. As usual, I can hear her breathing quicken with anticipation. I lick her again, massaging her bud with my tongue and she whimpers. I close my lips around her clit and suck on it lightly as if it were a delicate rose petal. You can't put your teeth on a rose petal or you'll mar it. She comes quickly, but I make her come a second time before I slide off the bed.

"Where are you going?"

"Get on all fours." She does as I say, but her face is pointed toward the headboard. "Turn this way."

She turns around so her face is in front of my hips and her ass is pointed at the mirror behind her. Perfect view.

I grab the hair on the back of her head and slide my cock into her open mouth. "Oh, yeah."

Like a good girl, she covers her teeth with her lips and lets me use my hips to decide how slow and fast I want it. Watching the mirror as I ease into her slowly, I smile when I see her hand reach between her thighs to touch herself.

Her muffled moans only get me more excited. I thrust into her just a little deeper until her eyes widen, then I pull back. I go back and forth between watching her face and watching her ass in the mirror. Then she pulls her hand out from between her thighs and I know she wants me to finish inside her.

I pull out of her mouth and she sits back. Then she beckons me forward until I'm settled between her legs. I kiss her deeply as I slide into her and finish her off missionary style.

I'm not totally opposed to missionary. I just happen to like my sex the way I like my hotel rooms. With a gorgeous view.

Besides, it's rare that I get the opportunity to satisfy my kinky cravings anymore. We had to tear down all the walls in the basement and get rid of the dance room and the dungeon after a water main broke and flooded the basement. It's been under construction for four months because we can only have the crews here when five-year-old Knox, Jr. is at school. Otherwise, he asks too many questions about what they're doing down there. And I'm trying to keep my construction plans for the basement a secret.

It's been hilarious for me to witness Rebecca's frustration since the dungeon flooded. She found as much release in there as I did. Probably more. She didn't need to be the always-in-control super-mom in the dungeon.

Now she casts dirty looks at the entrance to the basement whenever she passes. As if the basement is to blame for her sexual frustration. But I have a little surprise for her that I think will ease her tension a bit.

I come inside her and wait a moment before I roll over onto my back to catch my breath. "You wore me out, gorgeous."

"Yeah, right," she says, patting my abs. "Get up. We have a game to catch."

10

REBECCA

KNOX SNAGGED US some seats right behind the Yankee dugout at Yankee stadium. I don't know how he did it, but I've learned not to ask. When Knox and I decided he would not resume his identity as Marco Leone, I knew I would have to put up with the secrecy and mystery surrounding Knox Savage. I'm okay with that. Actually, it's one of the things I love the most about him.

Lita sits one seat away from me on my right, with three-year-old Ella between us and her little monster, ten-month-old Mason, in her lap. Eighteen-month-old Jade is in my lap and five-year-old Knox, Jr. is on my left, between Knox and me. Knox, Ella, and Jade. One boy and two girls. Knox wasn't ready to concede defeat. So I'm two months pregnant with boy number two.

I couldn't wait for the first ultrasound to find out this time. We got the Materni T21 blood test to find out the gender and make sure there were no chromosomal abnormalities. Not that I expected any of those. I really just wanted to know if Knox was going to get his second son. Because that means this will be my final pregnancy. Yay!

Lita hands me the bag of peanuts and Jade reaches for the bag. She's the only one of the kids with Knox's brilliant sky-blue eyes. Her dark hair is soft and wavy, and curls up at the ends, like mine. I love running my fingers through her hair when she falls asleep next to me.

I take a handful of nuts out of the bag and pass it down to Knox. I crack a peanut open and Jade's chubby hand reaches for the nut.

"No, sweetie. You can't eat those."

She grunts and mumbles something unintelligible. She's just learning how to talk and Knox insists that we pretend to understand what she's saying, the way we did when Knox and Ella learned to talk. Knox considers himself a child-rearing expert after reading two parenting books.

I reach into my purse and pull out a plastic baggie of digestive biscuits. "I brought you some cookies."

"Yuck!" Knox, Jr. says, scrunching up his face at the sight of the biscuits.

Jade looks at Junior then back at the baggie and shakes

her head. "No."

That's one word she knows how to say very well.

Junior slides off his seat and attempts to climb onto the railing. My heart nearly stops, but Knox's arm shoots up and grabs him around the waist.

"Sit down."

That's all Knox has to say and Junior immediately does as his father says. When I discipline him, I have to threaten to take away his toys and TV. And he still only listens to me about half the time.

We've made it through two innings, but I have a feeling this brood isn't going to make it much further. Ella keeps trying to touch Mason and I can see Lita getting frustrated. I thought I was over-protective when my kids were babies, but Lita is way worse than I was. She doesn't like to let anyone hold Mason unless they've washed their hands. Especially children.

Now Mason is starting to scream. It's time to leave before one of these angry Yankee fans says something Knox will make him regret.

"Well, two and a half innings is a record for us," I say as we wait on 161st for the cars to pick us up.

Lita and I take Mason and Jade in one car and Knox takes Ella and Junior in the other car. He makes fatherhood look way too easy. I guess it *is* a lot easier when your children regard you as a king.

"You're still going with us next week, right?" I ask

loudly so I can be heard over the sound of Mason's screams.

Lita is supposed to spend Easter weekend with us at my mom's house in East Hampton. Her husband, Gabriel Andreas (the third!), is supposed to be in Greece visiting his mother for Easter. Lita refuses to take Mason on an airplane; those cesspools of germs, as she likes to call them.

Gabriel and Lita met at an investor's meeting three years ago and they claim it was love at first sight. He's not as gorgeous as Knox, but he and Lita look like royalty when they're together. And it's almost sickening the way Gabriel dotes on Mason and Lita. The only reason he's leaving the country on Mason's first Easter is because his grandmother is very sick and this is likely her last Easter.

"Of course we're going," she replies, from the middle row of seats in the SUV. She looks over her shoulder at me and Jade and sighs when she sees Jade is already asleep in her carseat. She turns back to Mason and continues to try to soothe him. "I'm not flying with Mason until he's three. I don't care how many times Gabriel asks me to go with him in that sexy Greek accent."

The car turns onto Lita's street and Mason finally begins to settle down.

"Great! The car will pick you up Saturday morning. We have lots of fun stuff planned for the kids Saturday, then we'll have an adult dinner to celebrate Marie's birthday."

"Sounds fab."

The car stops in front of the twelve-story building on the Lower East Side where Gabriel and Lita enjoy a beautiful view of New York harbor. Knox and I still live in the townhouse, but we spend summers with my mom in the Hamptons.

My mom was more than willing to leave Bensonhurst, and all the memories, behind after my father's death. Sometimes I feel like she's happier now than I've ever seen her in my life. This makes me sad for my father, but also glad for my mother. After everything my father put her through, she deserves a quiet, peaceful life.

When Lita exits the car, Knox joins us in our car with Ella and Junior. Ella sits primly between me and Jade, and my two handsome men sit in the middle row of seats in front of us. The ride to grandma's house in East Hampton is quiet until Ella turns to me.

"Are we going to see Grandma Ella?"

We visited Ella Leone's gravesite a few weeks ago on the anniversary of her death. I was reluctant, but Knox insisted on bringing Junior and Ella with us so they could pay their respects. I was afraid the graveyard and the story of Grandma Ella would scare them; especially Ella, since they share the same name. But it had quite the opposite effect on her. She was fascinated by the graveyard and absolutely giddy at being named after someone. Since then, she's been asking when we're going back to visit Grandma Ella.

The innocence in her eyes melts my heart. "No, sweetie. We're visiting Grandma Marie today. And Grandma's making you some cupcakes and you're going swimming. Sounds like fun, doesn't it?"

She nods her head, though I can see a hint of disappointment in her eyes.

Ella's baby sister Jade looks like her father, but she also has his fiery temperament. Three-year-old Ella, on the other hand, is my angel. Always so peaceful and agreeable. When she first started walking on her own, she used to fall asleep at my feet while I was blowdrying my hair.

Two hours later, the car pulls into the gate at Grandma Marie's house. I lift Jade gently out of the car seat and Knox carries her inside. We find my mom in the kitchen. And she's not alone.

11

REBECCA

THERE'S A MAN in my mother's kitchen, standing at her shoulder, watching her pipe frosting onto a tray of cupcakes. And she's smiling. They're both smiling.

"Mom?"

She jumps at the sound of my voice and a large squirt of white frosting shoots out of the piping bag. Not the image I wanted to see right now.

"Rebecca! You scared the hell out of me."

"*I* scared *you*? What's going on here?"

She looks down at the messy pile of frosting on the counter and looks up innocently. "I'm making cupcakes for the kids."

I narrow my eyes at her then glance at her male companion. She can't help it. She's smiling like a schoolgirl with a crush.

Oh, no.

"Sweetheart, this is Kyle Mayer. *Dr.* Kyle Mayer."

She looks so proud of her *doctor* friend. But I feel like her pride is an affront to my father. As if now that he's gone, she can finally be with a *better* man.

"So nice to meet you, Rebecca." Dr. Kyle stretches his hand across the kitchen island toward me. I begin to reach for his hand, but Knox beats me to it.

"Nice to meet you, Kyle. I'm Knox Savage. Rebecca's husband."

Kyle looks taken aback by this, but I can't hide my smile. Knox has a weird thing about men who introduce themselves to me first. He hates it. Kyle is going to have to do something really nice to get on Knox's good side.

As if on cue, Kyle looks Knox in the eye and smiles. "Knox Savage? The same Knox Savage who just bought a piece of the Yankees?"

My eyes widen as I turn to Knox. His lips curl into the signature half-smile and I smack his arm.

"You didn't tell me you were buying the Yankees!"

He shakes his head. "Just a piece." He turns to me and nods toward his shoulder where Jade is asleep and slobbering all over his shirt. "Can you put her down so Kyle and I can chat?"

I reach out and he lays her gently in my arms. He kisses Jade's forehead and me on the lips. Then he takes

Junior and Ella by the hand and coaxes Kyle outside so they can talk.

My mom looks worried as she watches them leave through the back door. She knows Knox is going to have a man-to-man talk with her new boyfriend and there's nothing she can do about it. Finally, she tears her gaze away from the door and follows me upstairs.

I lay Jade down in the crib in the baby room. Smoothing her hair away from her forehead, I lay a soft kiss on her sweet baby skin and her wispy eyebrows shoot up. That's one of my favorite things about babies; when their eyebrows shoot up while they sleep. *What are they dreaming about?* Knowing Jade, she's probably dreaming about her daddy.

I pull up the rail on the crib and turn on the baby monitor before I meet my mom in the hallway. "You want to tell me who the hell Kyle Mayer is? I mean, it would have been nice to know you were having company before we brought the kids over."

"Oh, please, Rebecca. Kyle isn't spending the night here. He's just having dinner with us."

I watch her descend the curved staircase ahead of me and she's swinging her hips like a bell. "Mom! I've never even met this guy and you're inviting him over to spend time with my kids? Don't you think you should have introduced him to us first? At least let me decide if I want to leave my kids here with a strange man?"

"For God's sake, Rebecca. Listen to yourself. Do you really think I would let anything happen to my grandchildren?"

We reach the bottom of the stairs and I follow her back into the kitchen where she proceeds to finish icing the cupcakes. If my father were here, he would take a taste of the frosting and proclaim it too sweet, all the while smiling as he took another swipe at the frosting.

My stomach aches whenever I think of my father. Six years and I still miss him. I still regret never saying goodbye to him.

I know my mother's relationship with my father was very different, but I know they loved each other at some point. She deserves to move on and find happiness, but I don't know if I'm ready to watch it happen.

I watch silently as she continues piping the frosting onto the tiny cakes, thinking of the trip we took to Italy six years ago to scatter my father's ashes in Lago Di Bilancino. My father swam in that lake as a kid and his will was very short with explicit instructions. He left everything to my mother and he wanted his ashes scattered in the lake where he spent the happiest moments of his childhood.

After the ceremony on the lake, Knox and I spent some time in Florence where Knox tended to my every whim. He would walk down to the corner pasticceria every morning to buy me pastries and sandwiches to fatten me up. My job was to lie in bed and look pretty while he fed me and fed *on* me. I was only one-month-pregnant with Junior at the time, so we were both pretty nervous about me overexerting myself.

But we learned how durable I was when I was pregnant with Ella. And I've actually enjoyed being pregnant for most of the past six years. Sometimes, Knox will just look at my pregnant body and he'll get an instant erection. It feels good to have that kind of effect on him. But I'm looking forward to having more energy after this one is born. This is definitely our last child.

"Is Lita still coming next weekend?"

My mom wants to change the subject. I don't blame her. I don't really feel like talking about her boyfriend either.

People breakup and they move on and there's always something bittersweet about it. Even when August got a new girlfriend, I'll admit I was a bit jealous. Until I found out how they met. August will be getting married in East Hampton this summer to a professional sailor.

Sarah commented on August's blog post about vintage nautical fashion a couple of years ago, to berate August on his shitty taste. Sarah has sailed around the world twice; once when she was just fifteen and again when she was twenty-two. She's strong and beautiful and she calls August out on all his hoity-toity bullshit. In other words, she's perfect. So, yeah, I was a little jealous of her. But only for a few minutes. It's difficult to envy anyone when I have Knox.

"Yes. Lita's staying the night on Saturday," I reply. "But I wouldn't bank on her staying longer than that."

"She's still treating that baby like a bubble boy?"

I shrug, not willing to speak ill of my best friend with my mom today. "Mom?"

She looks up from the last cupcake she's icing. "What?"

"Don't forget Dad loved you."

She's silent for a moment, then she looks down at the cupcake. "I know, but your father had a strange way of showing it. And I think he would want me to be happy." She looks up again. "Don't you want me to be happy?"

I nod because I can't bring myself to say the words aloud. She sets down the piping bag and rounds the island so she can wrap her arms around my shoulders. I hug her back, swallowing the knot in my throat so I don't cry.

She uncoils her arms from around my shoulders, but her hands still grip my arms. "How could anyone forget your father? He was a great father. And, at one time, the best husband I could have imagined for myself. Your father and I lived a fairy tale when we were first married. I could never forget that. I *will* never forget that. I promise."

I look into my mother's brown eyes and I realize she is not the same person she was six years ago. Six years out of Bensonhurst and she looks and speaks differently. Everything about her looks lighter. I guess you can't carry the burdens of the past around forever.

Knox walks in with Kyle and the kids following closely behind him. "You ready to go, baby?"

I nod and we say goodbye to the kids. Junior is totally uninterested in us, as he's already gone straight for the video game console in the entertainment room. Ella is a little more difficult to leave behind.

"When are you coming back, Mommy?" she asks, clinging to my leg.

I scoop her up in my arms and hug her hard. "I'll be back in the morning, sweetheart. Daddy and Mommy are going to spend some time together for our third anniversary. It's a very special day."

"Can I come with you? *Please?*"

This is always the hardest part.

"No, sweetie. Not this time. But I'll take you to the park tomorrow and we'll spend all day there. Okay?"

She's still pouting, but she nods reluctantly. I squeeze her so tight she giggles, then I set her down and kiss her forehead. I leave the house quickly, before I can change my mind about leaving the kids behind. Knox and I hop into the back of the car together and the driver sets off out of the driveway and through the gate.

Knox drapes his arm over the back of the seat and I pull it down around my shoulder so I can snuggle up with him. "It's just one night," he says, squeezing my shoulder. "They'll be fine."

"I know. But this better be a good surprise or I'm never doing this again. It's too hard."

He chuckles. "Oh, I wouldn't say it's a *good* surprise."

"What does that mean?"

"You'll see."

12

KNOX

REBECCA LAYS HER head in my lap and settles in for the two-hour drive back to Manhattan. All I want to do is touch her. I want to grab her breasts. They're so plump with pregnancy hormones. I love her body when she's pregnant. But I have to be patient. Sex is always better when you draw out the payoff.

And I have a huge payoff planned for tonight.

As we pass through Brooklyn, I can't help but think of my mother. Which inevitably leads to thoughts of Geneva and Tony. I haven't heard from Geneva in six years. Not that I expected to. But she's been a good girl and she's kept quiet about my identity. And in return, I've kept my word and I haven't had Tony murdered in prison.

I also set up an anonymous trust fund for Geneva's

son. My nephew, who will grow up without a father because of me. I still partly blame Tony for that. I never would have taken out Geneva's boyfriend Nico if I knew Geneva were my half-sister.

I thought I might have second thoughts about having Tony killed in prison after finding out the bastard is my biological father. But I don't. I still want to watch the motherfucker burn. But I'm nothing if not extremely patient.

I went for the long game when I lured Tony in. It took me ten years and I never regretted a second of it. And I'll wait another ten or twenty years, or however long it takes, until I think Tony has suffered long enough. Then I'll order the hit. I just can't stand the thought of Tony dying of natural causes after what he did to my mother.

I brush a long lock of hair off Rebecca's face and see her eyes are closed. She's always so tired during the first few months of pregnancy. When she was pregnant with Junior, she fell asleep at Billy's funeral. She was so embarrassed, but I thought it was adorable.

And she wasn't the only one who was out of it at Billy's funeral. Bruno was hopped up on pain meds after spending six days in the hospital for the gunshot wound that nicked his carotid artery and shattered his clavicle.

But Bruno's a tough kid. He was back at work a couple of weeks after the funeral. His aim isn't as good as it used to be, but he's still the only guy who knows what needs to be done before I say a word.

By the time we get to the Brooklyn Bridge, Rebecca is snoring softly. I almost consider telling the driver to take us home for a quiet evening alone, but I know she'll be pissed as hell tomorrow morning when I tell her what she missed out on. And I'd rather she save her anger for the bedroom.

Rebecca likes to complain about my temper sometimes, but she's got quite a bite herself. And she secretly loves the way I keep her on her toes. Three years ago today, two months after she gave birth to Ella, I had Rebecca abducted and flown to Paris for our surprise wedding. It took her four hours to forgive me for scaring the shit out of her and climb onto the altar. But it was the best decision she ever made. And how many women would die to say they were abducted by Knox Savage for a surprise wedding?

I reach forward and place my hand over Rebecca's abdomen, holding it there as she breathes in and out. Ultimately, Rebecca knows I'd never do anything to hurt her. And I'd never let anyone else hurt her. My world changed the day I proposed to her on the bridge. New York City became a different place.

Suddenly, everywhere I looked I saw something or someone who could hurt Rebecca or my children. I tried convincing Rebecca to move to the country with me, but she didn't seem interested in milking goats or learning to cook. She's too fucking spoiled. But that's what I love about her. She's my city girl, through and through.

And Junior's in a good private school. She said she'd consider moving to the Hamptons if the school turns out to be a dud. But she doesn't want to leave the city. She loves working for me.

Yes, Rebecca works for me now. Her law enforcement background came in handy when I created a new position for her at Knox Security: Research Analyst. She's supposed to report to my security analyst, but she reports to me instead. And by reports to me, I mean she comes into my office every now and then and drops her reports on the floor. Then I help her pick them up. We have a great working relationship.

I shake her shoulder gently as the car pulls up in front of the Knox Security building. She sits up and lets out a long sigh. She blinks a few times as she looks out the window.

"Why are we here?"

"I want to show you something before I give you your anniversary surprise."

Her shoulders slump. "Can it wait? I really don't want to go in there right now. I'm so tired."

"Can it *wait*?" I repeat her words back at her. "Is that the way you talk to your boss?"

She glares at me then steps out of the car. I try to suppress my smile as I step out after her.

13

REBECCA

KNOX RARELY CHASTISES me in the office. And he never reprimands me in front of anyone else. He believes that everyone at Knox Security should respect and fear me the way they do him. But in private, he can sometimes be a prick.

I know you don't become successful without having some form of perfectionism. You have to be really good at what you do to be in high demand. And Knox is extremely good at what he does. His ability to hide and protect people is unmatched by anyone else in the industry. He continually reminds me of this every time I screw up.

But he hasn't reprimanded me at work in months. Heck, it may even be more than a year since he last chewed me out over a mistake. So whatever I did to deserve a talking to before our anniversary surprise must have been pretty bad.

Somehow, I can't bring myself to care. But that's not what Knox is going to want to see. There is nothing that pisses him off more than apathy.

By the time we reach his office, I'm teetering between extremely nervous and supremely pissed. I stand in front of his desk in my black halter dress and silver sling backs waiting for my scolding, trying not to look too annoyed.

He stands behind his silver and black desk chair, eyeballing the tablet on the glass desktop. His smile reappears briefly as he reaches for the tablet. He taps in his passcode and turns the tablet around to face me. A mugshot of a heavyset Puerto Rican guy pops up next to the stats for a guy named Carlos Rivera.

"Do you recognize this guy?"

I try not to roll my eyes. "No. Who is he?"

"This is Carlos Rivera. He's been on the run for two years for conspiracy to commit murder. Do you know who he was planning on killing?"

I grit my teeth. "No. Who was he planning on killing?"

His nostrils flare as he begins losing his patience. "Me."

I let out a soft chuckle. "Yeah, right."

"You think I'm joking? Do I look like I'm joking?" He pauses for a moment, then he continues without giving me a chance to respond. "I told you yesterday that I had a very important case for you and what was your response?"

I think back to yesterday and it takes a moment to remember what I was doing. "It was the end of the day on Friday. I told you it would have to wait until next week because I was taking Jade to get her shots."

"So you think Jade's immunizations are more important than my life?"

"What? Are you—Did you seriously just ask me that?"

"Answer the question!" he roars.

I stare into his eyes for a moment, then I shake my head. "I am through arguing about this. The next time you give me an assignment this important, you be up front with me about it or I swear to God, Knox, I'll quit."

He cocks an eyebrow and chuckles. "You think that's it? You think you're getting off that easy?" I turn to walk out of his office and he grabs my arm. "Not so fast, Mrs. Savage. I don't think you've been properly punished for your bad judgment."

I spin around to give him a piece of my mind, when I notice the bookcase behind his desk slowly swinging backward. I watch, completely mesmerized, until it stops moving and I glimpse the blackness beyond.

"What's that?"

I recognize the hungry look in Knox's eyes when he responds. "Your penance."

14

KNOX

THE FEAR IN her eyes is a turn-on. But the fear quickly turns to excitement when I hit the light switch and she steps into the new dungeon.

The walls are a deep maroon color and silver drapes hang from the ceiling to floor, framing mirrors that are meant to look like windows. Hanging on the walls between each faux-window are various punishment tools: whips, paddles, brushes, feathers. Then there are the restraints: ropes, chains, cuffs, belts, and even a straitjacket. Gags and blindfolds are in the bedside table with various other toys.

There is one plush gray sofa at the far end of the room and a couple of armchairs flanking the entrance where we're standing. Up against the wall on the right stands a rolling "wheel of pain" with wrist and ankle straps. Just beyond that is a plain canopy bed with a regular mattress—no spikes—for recovery. But above the bed hangs an intricate suspension system, which I suspect we'll have lots of fun with in the future.

She turns to me after she's had a look around and she can't hide her excitement. "You had this planned all along?"

"Maybe."

"Is Carlos Rivera even real?"

"Yes, he is very real. And he *was* ordered to take me out." I press a button on my phone and the wall closes behind me. "But he'll never find me in here." Taking a step toward her, I slide my arm around her waist and pull her against me. "So I guess that means you still need to be punished."

Her breathing quickens as I brush my lips over hers. But she knows the rules. She's not allowed to kiss me unless I give her permission.

Keeping my lips pressed against her, I pull the skirt of her dress up and slide my hand between her legs. I smile when my fingers find the soft flesh, freshly-waxed and soaking wet.

"No panties. Such a good girl," I murmur in her ear as I press my thumb against her clit.

I pull back and tilt my head as I look at her face. Her eyes are closed, lips slightly parted, as if she's waiting for something. Removing my hand from between her legs, I reach up and slowly slide my thumb into her mouth. The corners of her lips turn up slightly as she sucks softly on my thumb.

"That's right, baby."

I slide my thumb out of her mouth and she opens her eyes. I shake my head and she quickly closes them again. Taking her hand, I lead her toward the bedside table.

"Strip."

She begins pulling her dress over her head as I pull a blindfold out of the bedside table. When I turn toward her, she's standing patiently with her eyes closed, trying not to smile. She's not wearing a bra.

I take her nipple between my index finger and thumb and squeeze, gently at first then a bit harder. She winces at the pain so I lean forward and take her nipple into my mouth to soothe her. She lets out a soft sigh as I trace my tongue in a light circle around her nipple.

I move behind her and tie the blindfold in place. Then I sweep her hair over her shoulder to expose her neck. I trace my fingertip lightly down the back of her ear and neck, smiling as goosebumps sprout over her shoulders. I continue down her spine until I reach her perfectly round hips. She's holding her breath as she waits for me to do something.

I lean forward and whisper in her ear. "Don't move."

Peeling off my shirt as I cross the room, I retrieve a length of rope and black wooden paddle from where they hang on the wall, then I tie her wrists low on the bedpost so she's forced to bend over. Leaning over her, I reach between her legs to find her clit. She whimpers as her knees begin to buckle.

"Are you comfortable, princess?"

"Yes."

"Yes...?"

She moans, trying not to collapse as I caress her slick bud. "Yes, Master."

Her legs tremble as I massage her slow and then fast, and I know she can't take much more before her legs turn to rubber and give out beneath her. I remove my hand from between her thighs and she gasps.

"Wait. Please don't—"

"I didn't say you could speak."

"But I—"

I switch the paddle to my right hand and swat her; not too hard, but enough to quiet her. Instantly, her legs straighten up so her ass is higher in the air. Her way of begging for more.

"Are you ever going to make me wait when I give you an assignment?"

"No, sir."

I trace the cool edge of the paddle over her round hips, then down the side of her thigh. "How many spankings do you think you deserve for such a grievous error?"

"Whatever you think I deserve. You're always right."

I glide the paddle between her legs. She lets out a desperate whimper as I move it gently back and forth between her folds. Just the sight of luscious ass and her moisture glistening on the paddle is getting me rock hard. I want to push myself inside her right now, but I must be patient.

Sliding the paddle out from between her legs, I land another soft swat on her backside. Her cheeks are getting a soft pink now. I caress her skin softly to soothe her and her breathing slows down as she relaxes. Four more swats and I toss the paddle to the floor.

I bend over her and twist my fingers through her hair to turn her head. My other hand reaches forward, grabbing her nipple and twisting until she lets out a soft squeal.

"Do you want more?" I whisper in her ear.

"More. Please."

"Please…?"

"Please, Master?" Her plea comes out high-pitched as I squeeze my fist around her hair. "Oh, my God," she pants.

I unbuckle my belt and unfasten my pants, and she screams as I push myself inside her. Another thing I love when Rebecca's pregnant is how she feels tighter. As if I needed any more reason to lust after her.

She's so fucking wet. She loves the paddle more than anything else. I pierce her slowly, watching my cock as it slides in and out of her perfect pussy. Then I grab her hair again and ride her hard. Letting her cries fuel my desire until I come like a fucking rocket blasting off inside her.

I untie her wrists and scoop her up in my arms so I can lay her down on the bed. It's recovery time. Now I get to take away all the pain and build her back up. I must admit, this is my favorite part.

15

REBECCA

MY ABDOMINAL MUSCLES and my arms ache from the tension and release. Not to mention the stinging on my skin. I let out a thankful sigh of relief when Knox lays me on my side on the cool comforter.

I love the paddle the most. It makes me feel like a naughty schoolgirl, which is my favorite fantasy. But I knew Knox would go easy on me today considering I was already so tired when we walked into our new dungeon. He's a very considerate master.

He retrieves a soothing balm from the bedside table and lies next to me so he can rub it over my cheeks. His hands are warm and firm as he smooths the balm over my skin. I just want to scoot back and melt into him.

"Does that feel better, princess?"

"Yes, sir."

He grabs my hip and pushes me forward so I'm lying on my belly. He rubs my back for a while, kneading the tension away until I'm completely relaxed. Then he moves down to my legs, lightly massaging the backs of my thighs. As his fingers whisper over the sensitive area where my thigh melts into my cheek, I feel myself becoming engorged with anticipation.

He grasps my hip again and turns me onto my back. His sky blue eyes are filled with a deep longing as he gazes down at me. Then his hand lands gently on my abdomen.

"Let's have one more after this one. Just one more."

I smile as I reach up and wipe the sweat from his brow. He turns his face into my hand and lays a soft kiss on the inside of my wrist. *How can I ever say no this man?*

"Are you afraid I won't be quite as appealing when I'm not pregnant?"

He leans forward and kisses my cheekbone. His hand travels down my abdomen, then he whispers in my ear. "You are beautiful whether you're pregnant or not pregnant. There is nothing and no one more appealing…" He traces the tip of his tongue across my top lip. "…than my princess."

His hand glides over my hip and around to my ass. He lightly drags his fingertips over my tender skin, just hard enough to get me even more aroused. Then he grabs my ass with his massive hand and pulls me onto my side so he can press his body against mine.

He rubs his cheekbone against mine and I can hardly breathe. I wrap my arms around his neck and drape my leg over his hip so he can enter me. His solid chest is pressed against mine as our bodies rock back and forth in unison. A sensual dance of healing and forgiveness.

He kisses me hungrily as he grinds his hips into mine. "Just one more."

I throw my head back and let out a throaty chuckle. He seizes the opportunity to suck on the hollow of my neck. Then his hand slides down between us so he can massage my clit as he moves in and out of me.

Each thrust compresses his finger against my flesh, like a greedy finger pressing a jackpot. And by the trembling in his shoulders, I can sense that we're both about to win this round.

"Oh, Knox," I breathe, my body shaking as I finally get the orgasm I was denied earlier.

His cock twitches as he lets go inside me. I close my eyes to savor the warmth of his manhood as it fills me up. I clench the walls of my pussy around his cock and he smiles. His cock continues to twitch as he softens inside me. I do this a few more times as I kiss him and drag my fingernails over his back. And soon he's hard again.

"I'll give you one more if you give me one more," I whisper in his ear.

"I can do better than that."

After six years together, I know there's nothing Knox wouldn't give me. And giving him one more child is hardly a compromise considering everything he does for me and the kids. And my mom. All he asks in return is that I belong to him. And that's hardly difficult. I love being his.

But I am not his possession. I am his fuse. I'm the fuse that lights him up. That keeps him ticking. He can't function without me and I'm useless without him.

From the moment he dragged me into that abandoned garage six years ago and I looked into those electric blue eyes, I knew my life would never be the same. I knew who he was the moment I felt that electric energy. I knew he was Marco.

"You don't know me, so don't bother sifting through those pretty little thoughts."

I smile as I think of those words he spoke to me six years ago.

No, I didn't know Knox Savage. I *made* him.

THE END

Continue onto the next page for a preview of
Unmasked #1 **by Cassia Leo.**

New York Times Bestselling Author

CASSIA LEO

UNMASKED

volume one

She was born into this world unwanted.
She will leave this world unmasked.

CHAPTER ONE

THE MONSTERS WE can't see are the scariest ones of all.

Six blocks and the guy walking on the opposite side of the street is still going in the same direction as me. I don't spook easily. I'm used to walking the streets at night. In fact, I only walk the streets at night. But something about this guy doesn't feel right.

I can't see his face.

This shouldn't scare me, since he can't see mine either, but being able to see another person's face naturally puts us at ease. This is one of the reasons some people despise talking on the phone. And also why I have had zero friends and boyfriends in all my nineteen years on this planet. No one ever sees my face. Ever.

Even when I applied for my job at the gas station. I

told the guy on the phone that I had a day job and I'd have to conduct the interview in the evening. Besides, I was applying for the nightshift position at the station. The guy bought it. The day job was a lie. The truth is, I don't go out during the day. I haven't been outside during daylight hours in years.

I don't have one of those diseases that make you break out in blisters when your skin is exposed to sunlight. My reasons for not allowing anyone to see my face in the light of day are much more vain than that, and it started the day I was born. My biological mother took one look at my face and begged them to take me away. I've been hiding ever since.

So it shouldn't make me uneasy that I can't see this guy's face, but something about the way his hoodie covers it and the fact that he never turns his head is giving me the creeps.

The gas station is in my sight now. Just a block and a half away. I can make it there.

The streets of downtown L.A. are crawling with all kinds of shady characters at night. It's like when you turn the lights out on a filthy apartment and all the cockroaches come out of their hiding places. The drug addicts and whores dominate. The homeless and the lost wanderers, picking through the garbage and looking for a place to lie down for the night. Then there's the drug dealers and gang members who try to lay low, but they have to come out and stake their claim and make their deals every once in a while.

Downtown Los Angeles is not a place where a scrawny nineteen-year-old girl like me should be walking the streets at night. But that's exactly why I do it. People see me walking down the street and they smile, thinking I'm an easy mark. They can rob me or rape me, maybe even murder me, and they'll get away with it. I won't put up a fight. But they don't know me. I'm far from easy.

The monsters we can't see are the scariest ones of all.

You probably think it's impossible for someone to be afraid of little ol' me when I'm walking these streets, but you'd be surprised. Our face is what we show to the world. It's how we're recognized. It's how we're remembered. Our face is our identity. When you hide your face, you're hiding your identity, and this makes people very nervous. In our feeble little minds, the only people who hide their faces in public are criminals and clowns.

Everyone's afraid of clowns. Criminals, on the other hand, are either feared or revered.

Hiding my face is how I make it through the streets of L.A. without getting raped and murdered. Those who don't fear me are fascinated by me.

Well, that and the fact that there's always someone watching over me. He watches from a distance because he knows better than to get too close.

I haven't spoken to my father since I moved out eight

months ago. I've walked these streets every day since then and I've only seen him on a dozen or so occasions. But I know my father. He was black ops for the army until my mother made him quit when he was just twenty-eight. Now he has his own private investigation firm. I've only seen him following me in his silver Audi S4 a dozen times because that's how many times he *wanted* me to see him.

But even without my father watching over me, I can take care of myself. And no one knows that better than my father. He trained me.

I glance across the street at the guy in the hood and a gold Mercedes SUV drives by for the second time since I left the house six minutes ago. Now I'm even more nervous. I can deal with just about any deadly situation thrown at me. But I can't outrun a car.

I glance around the familiar neighborhood, looking for an escape route in case the car is working with the guy across the road. The gas station is just a block away on the other side of the street. The guy in the hoodie will get there before me. So I can't bolt for it and barricade myself inside.

A strange chill passes over my skin as my instincts kick in. I should probably turn around, but I hate admitting defeat. I stop in the middle of the sidewalk, half a block from the gas station.

Then the gold Mercedes is back, but it's not coming for me. It cuts across the double-stripe painted in the middle of the street, driving against oncoming traffic, and pulls up next to the guy in the hoodie. A white Honda driving on the other side of the road blares its horn at the Mercedes. The shrill sound of the horn fades away as the guy in the hoodie approaches the Mercedes.

Bzzzzz. The soft buzz as the window rolls down on the Mercedes. The guy in the hoodie is fast. He pulls out a gun and shoots the driver of the Mercedes within a second of that window going down. From here, it sounded like a Desert Eagle .44 fitted with a supersonic suppressor. Not a very good silencer, but there aren't many options in silencers when you're packing that kind of firepower.

The guy in the hoodie opens the driver's side door and I can hear him grunt as he pushes the driver's dead body into the passenger seat. Then he drives off and pulls into the gas station. Shit!

I spin around and take off running back to my apartment. I race down Hope Street with a speed that would make some Olympic athletes envious. I'm a well-trained weapon. But one of the most important lessons my father taught me is that sometimes your best weapon is your ability to run.

Nothing on my body moves. My hood doesn't fly off exposing my hair. My sunglasses don't bounce on my face. Every bit of my disguise remains in place as I fly down the streets of L.A. like a black phantom. Black hoodie. Black jeans. Black sunglasses. All hiding a ghostly face that would send children screaming.

My eyes close in on a group of three guys coming out of a liquor store a block ahead. Their eyes immediately lock on me, as if they're waiting for me. They *really* don't want to get in my way right now.

Get out of the way, assholes.

I want to shout this at them, but I'm not a vocal person. I'll talk to someone at the gas station if they have a problem with their credit card or if they need directions, but mostly I keep quiet. I don't talk to my neighbors. I don't talk to store clerks when I go to the grocery store.

I don't talk to people because I don't like answering questions. I don't care if my appearance makes people nervous and they need to ask questions just to feel more at ease around me. If you don't feel at ease around me, fuck you. That's not my problem.

Oh, now they're standing shoulder to shoulder to block my path on the sidewalk. Stupid move.

The one on the left is wearing a white T-shirt that comes down to his knees to cover up the fact that his jeans are slung low enough to show his ass. The other two are just clones of him in different sizes. Shorty. Fatty. Stocky.

I rush Shorty at full speed, ramming my shoulder into his gut and sending him skidding across the concrete on his ass. Fatty and Stocky come at me from behind. I reach my hands back, crossing my wrists as I grab their noses. Then I twist around and ram their heads into each other.

Shorty gets off his ass and comes at me with a knife. I try to kick it out of his hand, but he steps back and I miss.

Always attacking, my father's reminder rings in my head.

Fatty grabs the back of my hoodie and a good chunk of the ponytail underneath. I reach to gouge his eyes as he yanks me backward. I stomp on his foot, then I grab his hand and pull him between me and Shorty. I bend his hand back and bring my elbow down on his forearm, breaking his arm bone. He drops to his knees as Shorty comes at me with the knife again.

"Hey, bitch!" Shorty says, holding the knife up as he approaches me. "You look like a freak, but do you *fuck* like a freak?"

He pulls the knife back, ready to strike. I wait until the last moment, just as he drives it forward toward my abdomen, before I pull my leg up and deliver a blow to Shorty's jaw that will no doubt have broken at least half his teeth and possibly rattled his brain enough to kill him. He hits the concrete with a sick thud, his knife clanging over the sidewalk and into the gutter.

Fatty tries to get up again, but I land a devastating blow to his ear. Stocky is still dazed, clutching the light pole, from a single headbutt. Fatty spits curses at me as I run away toward my apartment.

I cut across the empty parking lot on Hope and 9th, then I dash across the street to my building on 9th Street. Blasting through the swinging glass doors, I head straight for the elevators on the right. Then I pass right by them. Once I enter the door leading to the fire escape stairwell, I can breathe. But I still have four flights of stairs before I make it to my third floor apartment.

I burst through the door onto the third floor, my hand on my knife holster, fully expecting someone to already be here waiting for me. But there's no one here. I race down the drab gray corridor and stop in front of apartment 312. I get my key in the lock and my body inside the apartment in less than five seconds.

Darkness.

Sigh.

I'm home.

Then my mother's voice echoes in my mind again, warning me. *The monsters we can't see are the scariest ones of all.*

I've always hated my mother's voice. Even when I'm only hearing it in my mind. Even when it's giving me sound advice. I hate it. So high-pitched, so clear and crisp it sounds computer-generated. It's no wonder my father is completely insane.

I'll let you decide whether the same description can be applied to me.

I don't need to turn the light on to find my way into the kitchen. I live in the darkness. My eyes can adjust to darkness in less than two seconds.

My father put my body through every physical test he went through when training with the army. And a few he made up himself, like the night vision test, which involved shining a bright light in my eyes then turning off the lights right before he would attack me. But the night vision test was unnecessary. Because my left eye has an extraordinary ability to adjust to darkness.

And I live in the darkness.

Unfortunately, judging by the painful throbbing in my side and the tickling sensation of something damp running down my skin, I'm pretty sure Shorty stabbed me. I'll have to turn on the lights to get a good look at it.

I press the button on the range hood to turn on the light above the stove. There are four bulbs in the hood, but I took out three. I only need one. Lifting my damp black hoodie, I see my white camisole is soaked in blood from just beneath my breast and down all the way to my waist.

The hole in my camisole is right over the fleshy part of my side, though I'm pretty lean so there's not much flesh to spare there. I lift the camisole and find that the stab wound is about one and a half inches long. It's not spurting blood, but it's gushing pretty steadily.

Fuck.

I turn around to the kitchen counter behind me and pick up the old-fashioned telephone with the curly cord. Other than my laptop, which I rarely use, I don't do technology. I don't like anything that transmits a signal. Maybe that makes me a paranoid kook, but the bottom line is that I want to be able to disappear without a trace at a moment's notice. And cell phones, tablets, credit cards, all that crap is what gets you caught.

Case in point: Shorty. I may very well have killed him tonight. It doesn't matter that it was self-defense. I don't want even the possibility of a manslaughter trial in my future. If he's dead, his friends saw me kill him. There's a good possibility they'll find me. I could be arrested at any moment.

I dial the phone number for the gas station and Aasif picks up on the first ring. "Hello?"

He sounds stressed. I hope the guy in the hoodie didn't drop the Mercedes guy's dead body in the gas station parking lot. Aasif would not like that. He hates dealing with the police.

"Aasif, it's Alex. I can't make it into work today. I'm not feeling well."

"What's wrong? Are you dying or something?"

I force a small chuckle. "No, just a really bad stomach ache. I'm going to try to rest and see if it will go away. If not, I'll definitely have to see a doctor in the morning."

"For a stomach ache?"

"A really bad stomach ache."

"This is a really bad night for you to call in sick, Alex. I have police crawling all over here, treating me like a fucking terrorist."

"Just stay calm, Aasif. Don't give them a reason to

Rodney King you."

"Fucking racist pigs," he mutters under his breath.

"Aasif, I'll call you tomorrow to tell you if I'm better."

"Okay, see you tomorrow."

He hangs up and I immediately grab a spoon out of the drawer on the left. Then I turn up the flame on the stove. I pull the sleeve of my hoodie over my right hand, using it like a pot holder to protect my skin as I hold the spoon directly on the flame. When the spoon begins to glow, I pull it off the flame and immediately press it against the knife wound.

I try to hold it in, but a wretched moan escapes my lips. *Oh, God. Please let the wound be sealed.*

I pull the spoon away, taking some of my skin with it, and the blood is still trickling. Not gushing. But trickling is still too much.

A few tears roll down my face as I realize I have to get another spoon and do it again.

Bang. Bang. Bang.

At the sound of the knocking on my door, my hand flies up to turn off the stove light. I pull my shirt and hoodie down over the knife wound and slip my custom Ontario 498 army knife out of its holster at the back of my waist. Then I wait.

The sensation of the blood trickling down my skin is now more distracting than the pain in the wound or the burn. I'm used to pain.

Forty seconds. Forty-one. Forty-two. Forty-three.

Bang. Bang. Bang.

CHAPTER TWO

I STARE AT the door for a moment, then I force myself to move. My legs feel a little weak as I move toward the door. It's the loss of blood. If this is one of those guys coming to finish me off, I'm dead. I can't fight them off like this.

"What do you want?" I shout from where I stand off to the side of the door.

"Ma'am. This is Detective Rousseau, LAPD."

"I'm sleeping."

"Ma'am, I need to talk to you about a possible murder you saw on Hope Street. Can you please open up?"

A fucking detective. And he got here pretty fast if he just responded to the scene at the gas station. Aasif must have given him my address.

Unless he's not a detective at all.

"I didn't see anything."

"That's not what your boss said. We think you might be in danger. Please open up."

I almost laugh out loud at that one. They think I might be in danger, which is why they sent just one detective to protect me. This guy is a bad liar.

"Come back tomorrow." *When I'll be long gone.*

"Ma'am, this is quite urgent. If you don't open up, I'll be forced to secure a warrant to search your home. I don't want to do that. I know you didn't have anything to do with this crime or the other crime scene on Hope and 7th."

What the fuck? Now he's threatening to pinch me?

I glance at the window on the other side of the living room, covered in thick black-out curtains. I can't jump from three stories up. Maybe I can climb down the side of the building with my bare hands if there are no other cops or detectives out there. But I'm already weak from the loss of blood. If I lose my grip...

"My electricity got cut off. It's very dark in here."

"That's okay. I have a flashlight."

Of course you do.

"Just a minute."

I grit my teeth against the pain as I walk into the tiny utility closet where the stackable washer and dryer, a tankless water heater, and the electrical panel are kept. I flip the main switch on the electrical panel, cutting off all electricity to the entire apartment.

I shut the door to the utility closet and head to the door. Looking through the peephole, I'm not surprised to see a person in a black hoodie and dark jeans. His face is cloaked in shadow as he stares at the doorknob, waiting for me to answer.

Detective Rousseau. I didn't know detectives were in the business of killing people and witnesses these days.

I plant my feet firmly as I stand to the side of the door. Then I tighten my grip around the handle of my knife and tuck it behind my back. I'll pull this door open and the moment this guy makes a wrong move, he's dead.

I don't like using my knife in a fight. My father trained me in Krav Maga, so I know that any weapon I carry can be used against my opponent *and* me.

Disarm. Disable. Disengage. Those are the three steps my father taught me.

First, you disarm your opponent. Then, you disable them. That could mean anything from stunning them, knocking them out, or killing them. Finally, you disengage. You get the fuck out of there.

I turn the doorknob slowly, then I quickly swing the door inward while maintaining my cover behind the wall. The white beam of the flashlight pierces through the darkness, mostly diffused except for the small circle of light on the black armchair against the wall.

"Turn off the flashlight."

"Pardon me?"

He attempts to step inside and I jut my foot out to stop him. "Detective?"

There's a long pause. He knows I know he's full of shit.

A soft click and the beam of light recedes into the dimly lit corridor. "Better?"

His voice sounds different with the door open. There's a slight accent, but I can't tell if it's European or Canadian French. It doesn't matter. He's in my territory now. If he survives, he won't have a voice left to speak.

"Much better. Come in, Detective."

I keep my head bowed low so he can't see my face, but he moves slowly. He's trying not to provoke me. We'll see how long that lasts.

"I'm going to come in very slowly," he assures me when his right foot is completely inside. "No need to be alarmed."

I'll decide when it's time to be alarmed.

His body moves forward slowly and I finally glimpse the top half of him. He's holding both his hands up on either side of his face. One hand still clutching his flashlight; a very deadly weapon in trained hands. But his hood is still pulled up. And from this side angle, with his hands up, I still can't see his face.

Maybe that's a good thing.

I step to the right, farther away from the doorway.

"Close the door," I order him.

He takes another step forward so that now I can only see his back. Then he uses his foot to push the door closed. Total darkness.

"Keep your hands in the air and tell me who you really are."

The silence that follows my command is complete. He knows I'll be able to hear every move he makes in here. And he's right.

Since I was pulled out of public school at the age of six, my parents kept me locked away like a princess in a tower. Afraid that others would judge me the way the children and school staff had. They wanted to protect me. Or so they claimed.

My father trained me in the basement of our craftsman style 1920s house in L.A. Houses like that are rare in Southern California. They're worth a lot of money now. And my parents have sure mortgaged the shit out of that house. Hence, the reason I no longer live with them. They wanted me to start working for my dad's agency without getting paid. Of course, I'd still have to live in their dingy basement. Then there's also the whole thing with my mom being crazy and manipulative.

I hold my breath as I stare at *Detective* Rousseau's silhouette through the darkness. I don't think he's breathing. I wait another moment, thinking that if he doesn't speak or move soon I'm going to stab him in the jugular. Then I hear a soft intake of breath.

"I just need to know what you saw, so I can record your statement in my report."

He's still going to pretend to be a detective. Fine. I can play that game.

"I didn't see anything. So if that's the only reason you're here, I suggest you leave."

He sniffs the air softly as he turns around to face me. "Are you okay, Miss…?"

"I'm fine."

"I smell burned flesh."

"You know the scent of burned flesh?"

"In my line of work, I've come to know the scents of many things." He takes a step toward me. "Some pleasant and some not so pleasant."

I hold my ground. "Your line of work? They allow you to dress like that in your line of work?"

"I'm a detective. I don't wear a costume like those other clowns."

He's no more than five feet away from me now, his hands still up in the air and his flashlight in hand. His black hoodie still pulled up over his head. Combined with his black pants, he does a good job of blending into the darkness. Still, I have two advantages here. My left eye and the fact that I know I have an advantage in the dark. Knowing you have an advantage is half the battle, because nothing is stronger than confidence.

If I wanted to, I could close that five-foot gap between us, reach forward, and tear out his esophagus in one second flat. If I were operating at full power. But I'm not. And he can smell it.

He can smell my burned flesh. He can smell my weakness from five feet away. And he wants me to know. But why? Why not just pounce on me and finish me off? Why not just pull out that fucking .44 and blast me between the eyes?

Because he wants something. Everybody wants something. And whatever this guy wants, he needs me alive to get it.

"You refer to your fellow officers as clowns?" I reply, trying to color my voice with some mock disgust.

He chuckles and the sound sends a chill through me. "I'm not an officer. I'm a detective. I had to use my brain to get to this position, just like I had to use my brain to get your boss to tell me where you live."

I want to shout, *"You killed that man!"* but that would be very stupid of me. Instead, I maintain my composure as he takes another step toward me, closing the distance between us to no more than three feet.

"Are you going to tell me what you saw? Or should I come back tomorrow after you've had some rest?"

He's giving me an out. *Why?*

"You killed that man." I speak these words calmly, almost conversationally.

Through the darkness, I can see and feel his muscles tense. "That man was following you."

He's not even going to deny it. I don't know if I should be more frightened or impressed.

"No, he wasn't," I reply.

"Yes, he was. He is—was a known sexual predator. I've been following his case and waiting for him to strike. You were going to be his next victim."

"I don't believe you."

"Well, he's been watching you for a few days. And he certainly didn't appreciate me trailing you tonight. Which is why he pulled up next to me and attempted to shoot me. I shot him first."

I let out a puff of shrill laughter. "Oh, that's a good story. I'm sure it will make headlines."

He gazes at me, completely silent and still. Though I know he can't see me through the darkness, especially with my makeup and sunglasses and the hood over my head, I can't help the nervous feeling building in the pit of my belly. Something tells me playtime is over.

"I'll come back to speak to you tomorrow." He turns to head for the door. He stops as he places his hand on the doorknob. "Thank you for your time, Miss…?"

"Alex. Just Alex."

"Thank you for your time, Alex." He twists the doorknob and my body tenses as I await the soft glow of the lights in the corridor. But he doesn't open the door.

He looks over his shoulder and, even through the darkness, I can see the soft shadow of a smug grin on his face. "You should get that stab wound looked at by a physician." He reaches into his back pocket and I brace myself for a gunshot. But all he pulls out is a business card. "This community clinic will take care of you free of charge. No questions asked. Just tell them Detective Rousseau sent you."

Unmasked #1 by **Cassia Leo.**

http://bit.ly/unmaskedseries

OTHER BOOKS BY CASSIA LEO

CONTEMPORARY ROMANCE

Relentless (**Shattered Hearts #1**)

Pieces of You (**Shattered Hearts #2**)

Bring Me Home (**Shattered Hearts #3**)

Abandon (**Shattered Hearts #3.5**)

Black Box (**stand-alone novel**)

PARANORMAL ROMANCE

Parallel Spirits (**Carrier Spirits #1**)

EROTIC ROMANCE

Unmasked Series

KNOX Series

LUKE Series

CHASE Series

COMING SOON

Chasing Abby (*Shattered Hearts* **#4**)

GET INVOLVED

RATE IT: If you enjoyed this book,
please consider leaving a review wherever you
purchased it or at *Goodreads* (bit.ly/knoxseriesgoodreads).

JOIN US: Follow Cassia on *Facebook*
(http://on.fb.me/XrRo0c) and *Twitter*
(http://bit.ly/cassialeoTWT). Sign up for email updates on
Cassia's blog (http://bit.ly/cassianews) or become part of
her *street team* (http://bit.ly/cassiateam) to get inside
information on new releases, exclusive street team
giveaways, and more.

ABOUT THE AUTHOR

New York Times and *USA Today* bestselling author Cassia Leo loves her coffee, chocolate, and margaritas with salt. When she's not writing, she spends way too much time watching old reruns of *Friends* and *Sex and the City*. When she's not watching reruns, she's usually enjoying the California sunshine or reading—sometimes both.

8301231R00203

Printed in Great Britain
by Amazon.co.uk, Ltd.,
Marston Gate.